P9-CMX-449

"I'm not capable of running a Christmas tree farm."

"What?" Hawkins took a step back. "Have you forgotten about our collaboration? Our agreement?"

"It doesn't matter." They hadn't signed a formal agreement yet, anyway. "Even my two-thirds of the trees are still too much."

He dipped his head, urging Annalise to look at him. "You do realize we're playing catch-up right now. But we will catch up. Once we do that, the maintenance won't be near as overwhelming."

"There were six of us working today and we barely made a dent." To her chagrin, tears fell again, and she turned away.

After a moment, he moved in front of her. "I have no doubt that you *can* do this, Annalise. You've got my entire family excited about this endeavor. Including me."

His words washed over her like a healing balm, soothing her disbelieving heart. No one had ever spoken such encouraging words to her before. Though she couldn't help wondering if Hawkins truly believed what he was saying or if he was simply placating her.

Award-winning author **Mindy Obenhaus**
lives on a ranch in Texas with her husband,
two sassy pups, and countless cattle and deer.
She's passionate about touching readers with
biblical truths in an entertaining, and sometimes
adventurous, manner. When she's not writing,
you'll usually find her in the kitchen, spending
time with family or roaming the ranch. She'd
love to connect with you via her website,
mindyobenhaus.com.

Visit the Author Profile page at LoveInspired.com.

A Christmas Bargain

Mindy Obenhaus

LOVE INSPIRED
INSPIRATIONAL ROMANCE

If you purchased this book without a cover you should be aware that this book is stolen property. It was reported as "unsold and destroyed" to the publisher, and neither the author nor the publisher has received any payment for this "stripped book."

LOVE INSPIRED®

INSPIRATIONAL ROMANCE

Recycling programs
for this product may
not exist in your area.

ISBN-13: 978-1-335-58539-4

A Christmas Bargain

Copyright © 2022 by Melinda Obenhaus

All rights reserved. No part of this book may be used or reproduced in any manner whatsoever without written permission except in the case of brief quotations embodied in critical articles and reviews.

This is a work of fiction. Names, characters, places and incidents are either the product of the author's imagination or are used fictitiously. Any resemblance to actual persons, living or dead, businesses, companies, events or locales is entirely coincidental.

For questions and comments about the quality of this book, please contact us at CustomerService@Harlequin.com.

Love Inspired
22 Adelaide St. West, 41st Floor
Toronto, Ontario M5H 4E3, Canada
www.LoveInspired.com

Printed in U.S.A.

There is no fear in love; but perfect love casteth out fear: because fear hath torment. He that feareth is not made perfect in love.
—*1 John* 4:18

For Your Glory, Lord

Acknowledgments

To my wonderful husband, who truly is the inspiration for all of my heroes.

Chapter One

Excitement bubbled inside of Annalise Grant. Her new life was about to begin. A life lived on her terms, doing the things she loved, regardless of what anyone else thought. With the exception of the sixteen-month-old in her back seat. Her daughter, Olivia, had been growing fussier each and every mile of these last thirty minutes of their four-hour journey from Dallas. Still, Annalise kept smiling, knowing that once they were settled into their new home just outside of Hope Crossing, Texas, it would all be worth it.

Under a sunny, late-September sky, Annalise maneuvered her SUV into the parking lot of Plowman's, a quirky general store sort of place that served as a gas station, feed/hardware/grocery store and bakery. Her introduction to the unusual business had taken place some two months ago when she'd first visited the tiny town to survey the home and land her late husband's uncle had bequeathed to his heirs. And while her initial intention had been to sell the property, one glance had her quickly changing her mind.

Olivia whimpered behind her, no doubt tired of being held captive by her car seat.

"Just a minute, sweet pea." Annalise pulled into a parking spot. She needed to grab a few essentials before continuing on to their new home, a cute one-and-a-half story white farmhouse on almost fifteen acres, the majority of which were covered with Christmas trees. According to Uncle Gary's attorney, he and his wife, Eileen, had been on the verge of opening their Christmas tree farm prior to Eileen's untimely death last year. Yet while Gary had hoped to fulfill his wife's dream, sadly he, too, passed earlier this year.

Now, the house and the land belonged to Annalise and Olivia. And thanks to the detailed journals Gary and Eileen had painstakingly maintained, Annalise hoped to pick up where they left off.

She turned off the engine and stepped out into the afternoon sun, smoothing a hand over her sleeveless blouse and shorts. The humid air sifted over her bare arms, quickly warming her skin.

Opening the back door, she freed Olivia from her restraints and kissed her chubby cheek before setting her sparkly-pink-sandaled feet upon the pavement. With one hand on her daughter, she grabbed the diaper backpack that doubled as her purse from the floorboard and slung it over her shoulder before tossing the door closed.

The breeze caught Olivia's wispy dark blond hair, standing it on end as Annalise locked her vehicle. "Hold Mommy's hand."

Inside the compact store, the aroma of yeasty dough mingled with the sweetness of fresh-baked cookies and pies.

Her hunger awakened, Annalise grabbed a small cart and slipped Olivia into its seat. She quickly located the milk, eggs, bread, cereal and peanut butter that were on her list. That should be enough to hold them over until the movers finished unloading their furniture and other household items tomorrow. Then they could make a trip to the nearest supercenter to sufficiently stock the pantry, refrigerator and freezer.

Yet as Annalise eyed the bakery on her way to the checkout counter, a clear plastic container of chocolate chip cookies couldn't be ignored, so she added it to her cart as stealthily as possible, in case Olivia spotted them and demanded one right now.

At the one and only checkout lane, she placed the items on the counter, noting the long, tall drink of cowboy behind her. His faded jeans were covered in dust, as were his worn square-toed cowboy boots. Not to mention his maroon Texas A&M T-shirt and matching ball cap. His dark eyes scanned the place as he waited patiently to purchase a container of lunch meat and some funky-looking pliers, or whatever tool that was in his hand.

Olivia rubbed her eyes and began to fuss as the cashier rang up their total and bagged the items.

Annalise unzipped the front pocket on the diaper bag to retrieve her wallet. "Easy, sweet pea. We're almost done." Save for an old pacifier she kept for emergencies, the pocket was empty.

She slid the bag from her shoulder and, with a bit of frustration, rummaged through the large center compartment where she kept diapers and extra clothes for Olivia. But there was no wallet to be found. Or in any of the other three pockets.

Anxiety welled inside of Annalise as she eyed the cashier. "I think I left my wallet in the car. Can I pay with my phone?"

"No, ma'am. We're not set up for that here."

Annalise's gaze scanned the rather rustic place. "In that case, would you mind if I—"

"I got it, Diana."

Annalise jerked her gaze to the cowboy's as he passed a twenty spot to the cashier. The last thing she needed was someone sweeping in to save her. People had done that all her life, and she'd learned the hard way that, while their intentions might be good, it wasn't always in her best interest. "That's not necessary. I can—"

Olivia picked that moment to release a blood-curdling scream they could probably hear in the next county.

Twisting to face her daughter, Annalise said, "What is it, baby?" Following the child's outstretched arms, Annalise realized Olivia had spotted the cookies.

"Ookee." Tears pooled in her daughter's blue eyes, her face a brilliant red.

"In a minute, sweetie." She glanced from Olivia to the cashier to the cowboy, her own cheeks heating. "I'm sorry." Wishing there was a rock she could crawl under, she lifted her daughter from the cart. "Excuse us." Holding tightly to a still-screaming Olivia, she hurried out the door and back to their vehicle.

"It's okay, sweet pea."

Olivia shrieked even louder. "Ookee! Ook*ee*!" She twisted, and Annalise tightened her hold as her daughter aimed her outstretched arms back to the door they'd just exited.

Since becoming a mother, Annalise had been the victim of several embarrassing moments, but this one had to take the cake.

"Calm down, sweetheart." She opened the door to the back seat. "How about some crackers?" She snagged the zip-top baggie from the grocery sack on the seat.

Olivia adamantly jerked her head in the opposite direction. Leaving Annalise with only one option. She had to find that wallet.

Holding her daughter snugly against her hip despite the child's efforts to escape, Annalise scoured the back seat and floorboard but found nothing. She emerged into the heat and humidity once again, eager to check the front seat, when the cowboy who'd been behind her in line approached holding two white plastic bags.

"I believe you forgot something." He held them out.

"Ookee." Olivia's wails had morphed from earsplitting to pathetic whimpers.

The compassion in the cowboy's dark eyes made the lump that had already formed in Annalise's throat grow even larger. "Thank you." Mortified, she took hold of the bags. "I, uh—" she cleared her throat "—I *can* pay you, though." Turning, she struggled to open the front door.

He reached around her and opened it for her.

"Thank you." With Olivia in one arm and the bags dangling from the other, she eased onto the seat. "Just give me a minute to find my wallet."

Holding up both hands, he said, "That won't be necessary."

"But—" Before she could get the remaining words out, he nodded, turned on his heel and headed back into the store, leaving Annalise to deal with her flailing emotions.

After unpacking a cookie for her daughter, she placed the now-happy child in her car seat and resumed the search for her wallet until a dreadful thought played across her mind.

They'd made a pit stop a little over an hour up the road where she'd purchased a bag of nuts for herself and a toy for Olivia. And since her daughter had been on the verge of a meltdown, though not nearly as bad as the one just now, Annalise's focus had been on her.

Could she have left her wallet there?

After another frantic search of her SUV, she feared her worst-case scenario had become a reality.

Desperately in need of some heat relief, she started the engine, closed the door, then grabbed her phone and did a quick search for the convenience store in Lexington. Seconds later, she tapped the icon to call. After several rings, her angst ratcheting with each one, someone answered.

"Hello. My name is Annalise Grant. I was in your store about an hour and a half ago and purchased some snacks. Now I can't find my wallet. By any chance did you find a bright pink wallet somewhere?"

"Yes, ma'am. It was sitting right here on the counter, next to the container of miniature teddy bears."

Annalise eyed the purple one lying atop her dashboard. Olivia had sent the little critter flying through the air when they were only a few miles down the road.

She released a sigh. The thought of driving for two-and-a-half more hours was about as appealing as an ice bath in the middle of a winter storm. But she had no choice. "I'll be there in a little over an hour."

Ending the call, she eyed her dashboard. Only a quarter tank of gas. Not enough to get her back to Lexington. Or at least she assumed. Her model of SUV was known to have excellent gas mileage. But did she really want to risk it with a toddler in the back seat?

She shoved her hair away from her face. Could this Monday get any worse?

Just then, she saw the cowboy exit the store. Bag in hand, he paused and looked her way.

Oh, how she wished she could disappear.

She shrank into her seat as he started her way. Obviously, she was still visible.

Straightening, she stepped out to meet him.

"Everything all right?" The man she guessed to be a

smidge older than her thirty-two years eyed her daughter through the tinted glass.

"My daughter is, thanks to you. The cookies were a lifesaver."

His quick smile seemed to transform his face. "Glad I could help."

She raked her fingers through her shoulder-length hair, trying to ignore how incredibly handsome he was, despite the coating of dust. The close-cropped dark hair that was barely visible with his hat and the shadow of a beard that highlighted a strong jawline and chin. "The good news is that I located my wallet."

His dark brows lifted, disappearing under the brim of his hat.

"The bad news is that I left it in Lexington."

"That's more than an hour away."

"Yes, it is." She wished the earth would swallow her up as her next words formed on her tongue. The last thing she wanted was to be beholden to anyone, least of all a handsome stranger. But at the moment, she didn't have a choice. She was the proverbial damsel in distress, sorely in need of a rescue. No matter how much it hurt her pride.

"Sadly, I don't have the gas to make it there, nor do I have any means to purchase any."

He watched her for a long moment, and the skepticism she saw in his eyes was about the most embarrassing thing she'd ever experienced.

"I'm new to Hope Crossing, but if you could help me out with some gas, I promise I will pay you back tomorrow."

He continued to ponder her with wary eyes. Finally, "Pull up to the pump, and we'll get you taken care of."

The breath she'd been holding whooshed out of her lungs. "Thank you. I can't tell you how much I appreciate this. And I *will* pay you back. Just give me your address or phone number."

"That won't be necessary."

"No, I insist."

He paused. "Let's just say I'm paying it forward. The next time you encounter someone in trouble, do the same for them."

"I will. Thank you so much."

She settled back into her vehicle and maneuvered it toward the pump, feeling a little bit lower than a slug. Coming to Hope Crossing was supposed to be a fresh start. Yet as far as fresh starts went, this one was starting off pretty rotten.

His mother always told him having a tender heart was a good thing. Not from where Hawkins Prescott stood it wasn't. It made him a target for every bleeding heart, particularly those with a pretty face.

And here he'd gone and done it again. Hadn't he learned anything from his debacle in Alaska? Even if his company hadn't transferred him to Texas, the humiliation alone would've driven him back home in short order.

Forget what happened at Plowman's yesterday. You'll probably never see that woman again.

Not true. She said she was new to town. And since Hope Crossing was barely a map-dot, everyone knew everyone else. That was, of course, if she was telling the truth.

She had a kid. Besides, it didn't cost you that much.

That part was true. A few groceries, necessities at that, and a tank of gas were nothing compared to what Bridget had cost him.

Country music played on the radio as he drove his truck down the two-lane road after lunch Tuesday. He scrubbed a hand over his face. *Forget about the woman. You've got bigger problems.*

He certainly did. With his sister, Gloriana, and her husband, Justin, who managed their family's ranch, away on their honeymoon, Hawkins was in charge of Prescott Farms for the week. And since he'd been away for several years, only managing to catch a few days here and there to visit his mother, he'd taken the time to drive the entire property yesterday to make sure things were as they should be. The way they'd been when he and his father worked the ranch together when Hawkins was a kid. The same way they'd been after his father's sudden death when Hawkins had to come back after graduating from A&M to run the ranch for several years.

Yesterday, though, he wasn't pleased with what he had found.

At some point during his absence, one of their neighbors had moved their fence, effectively stealing land from Prescott Farms for what appeared to be a bunch of Christmas trees. Not that he blamed his brother-in-law. Justin had only been with them for a few years. The fence was likely moved before he ever arrived. Now it was up to Hawkins to confront the landowner to find out what was going on.

For the second time in as many days, he slowly approached the drive of Gary and Eileen Winston, a pleasant couple they'd never had any problem with. Until now. If Hawkins remembered correctly, Eileen had passed away last year, so he needed to take care not to come down too hard on Gary. Though, he would reclaim what rightfully belonged to his family. Assuming the man was home today.

At the rusted mailbox, Hawkins turned into the drive as a white box truck emblazoned with the name of a moving company barreled toward him, leaving a cloud of dust in its wake. Interesting. Was someone moving in or out?

Only one way to know.

He veered to one side of the drive, allowing the truck to pass before continuing on to the farmhouse set away from the road, nestled between a couple of mighty oak trees. The house appeared to be well maintained, as did the three outbuildings, one of which was a rustic old barn. Though, as his truck bumped up the gravel drive, he decided the road could use a good grading.

Nearing the house, he did a double take. The dark blue Ford SUV parked there looked just like the one that belonged to the woman he'd helped yesterday. What would she be doing at Gary's? He and Eileen didn't have any children.

He glanced back at the moving truck that had just exited the drive. Had Gary sold the place?

Hawkins came to a stop alongside the SUV, turned off his truck's engine and stepped out into the warm afternoon air, his gaze drifting to the back of the house and the multitude of pine trees growing in neat rows beyond the detached garage.

Briefly removing his ball cap, he scratched his head. *What's up with all the Christmas trees?*

He continued along the sidewalk at the front of the pier-and-beam clapboard house, then climbed the three steps onto the wide wooden porch. A couple of white wicker rockers were separated by a small table to his right, while a few empty cardboard boxes lined the railing.

He knocked on the ornate wooden screen door that had been painted the same dark green as the shutters and trim.

Moments later, the door beyond the screen swung

open, and the pretty blonde from yesterday stood there dressed in cutoffs, a blue T-shirt and sneakers, with her baby on her hip. Surprise had her eyes widening while pink tinged her cheeks.

"How did you…" She was clearly as dumbfounded as he was.

Eager to clear the air, he said, "I'm looking for Gary Winston." He stepped out of the way as she pushed the screen door open to join him on the porch. She was a tiny thing. Maybe all of five-three, if he had to guess.

The child's big blue eyes similar to her mother's seemed to light with recognition when she saw him. Grinning, she patted her chubby little hands together. "Ookee."

Uh-oh. He hoped she wasn't about to have another meltdown.

"I…guess you haven't heard." The blonde moved her daughter to the opposite hip. "Gary passed away earlier this year."

Surprise rattled through Hawkins. "No, I wasn't aware." He supposed he should've checked with his mother. She knew just about everything that went on in Hope Crossing; however, he'd hoped to hold off on telling her about the fence until he had things resolved.

"Gary was my husband's uncle. We inherited the house and the land."

"I see." Mentally regrouping, Hawkins said, "Could I speak with your husband, then?"

She pressed her lips together, momentarily dipping her head before meeting his gaze. "Uh, no. He's also deceased. My daughter and I are the sole owners."

"You're—" Good thing it wasn't windy, because it wouldn't take much to knock him over.

Pull yourself together, Hawk. You're here to reclaim your land.

"Oh, before I forget." She reached for the door, glancing over her shoulder. "Wait here. I'll be right back."

Hands shoved in the pockets of his jeans, he eyed a couple of cardinals perched on the limb of a nearby oak tree, rocking back on the heels of his boots as a cow's bellow echoed from the pasture across the road. Things were getting more perplexing by the moment. Nonetheless, he was determined to get to the bottom of this.

When the woman finally returned, she extended her hand.

He looked down, spotting the money clasped in her palm. A few dollars more than he'd spent, if he wasn't mistaken.

"Thank you for taking pity on us yesterday." She drew in a shaky breath. "I'm not sure what we would've done without you."

His fingers brushed her soft skin as he took hold of the bills, igniting an awareness that hadn't been there before. He stared at her a moment.

Nope, not going there.

He folded the money and tucked it in his pocket. "Glad I was able to help. I take it you got your wallet back."

"Yes, and everything was just the way I'd left it."

"Good." He again met her gaze, promptly realizing how big a mistake that was. She had the kind of eyes that made you want to get lost in them. Like the glacial waters of an Alaskan lake.

"So it sounds like you're wanting to talk to the owner here, and, well, that would be me."

The woman's smile was so childlike and carefree he almost hated to tell her the reason for his visit. But Gary had stolen land from Prescott Farms and Hawkins aimed to get it back.

"I guess I should introduce myself." He straightened to his full six feet two. "My name is Hawkins Prescott. My family owns the ranch that butts up to the back of this property."

"Well, it's nice to meet you, Hawkins. My name is Annalise, and this is my daughter, Olivia."

As if on cue, the child sent him a goofy grin that made him chuckle.

Business, Hawk.

He cleared his throat. "The reason for my visit is that I was driving the fence line at Prescott Farms yesterday and noticed a portion of the fence that bisects our properties has been moved, and a good portion of those pines that were planted are on Prescott land."

"How is that possible? Like I said, no one has lived here since early this year."

"The fence wasn't moved any time in recent history. I've been living in Alaska for the last several years. I suspect it was done sometime after I left, and our ranch managers didn't know the land well enough to notice it."

For a moment, her countenance seemed to fall, though she quickly recovered. Lifting her chin, she said, "And how do I know you're not simply trying to get your hands on a portion of my property?"

Wait, was she seriously accusing him? "If you'd care to take a little walk, I'd be happy to show you."

"You realize I'm holding a baby. Not to mention I have a lot of unpacking to do." She motioned to the boxes behind him. "How far are we talking?"

He looked from her to the child. "No, walking probably isn't the best idea. I don't suppose Gary has a utility vehicle around here somewhere, does he?"

"Utility vehicle? You mean, like a truck or something?"

Annalise was definitely a city girl, making him wonder how she was going to fare out here in the country. By herself, no less.

"More like a cross between a golf cart and four-wheeler. Makes it easier to get around one's property."

"It's possible." She shrugged. "I've been too busy trying to get the house situated to check any of the outbuildings. Wait, I do recall seeing something like what you described when Gary's attorney was showing me around a couple of months ago. It's in the garage."

"In that case, shall we have a look?"

She hesitated. "How do I know you're not a serial killer or something?"

He couldn't help the laugh that slipped out. "Don't worry, I left my ax at home."

Her gaze narrowed, and he suddenly felt kind of sorry for her. A woman raising a child alone in today's crazy world had every right to be afraid.

"You know what? Never mind." He raised his hands and took a step back. "That was a bad idea on my part. I apologize."

"Oh, so now I'm just supposed to take your word that the fence has been moved?" She cocked her head, her golden blond waves skimming her shoulder. "Without any proof?"

He couldn't believe this. Though, he had to give her credit. The lady was no pushover. But he still wasn't going to be swayed by another pretty face.

"Come on." She started down the steps. "Let's see if we can find one of those vehicles you were talking about."

They rounded the corner of the porch, continuing on

to the red metal structure with two roll-up garage doors situated beyond the back corner of the house.

She took hold of the knob on the walk-in door to the left. When it refused to open, she reached into her pocket and pulled out a key ring sporting at least a half dozen keys.

After a couple of tries, she met with success.

Inside, she flipped the light switch as they entered, illuminating the large space that held not only a utility vehicle but a vintage red Ford pickup reminiscent of those used in Christmas photos, usually with a tree sticking out of the bed.

"Is that what you were referring to?" She pointed beyond the truck to the open-air vehicle with a bench seat, roof and a small bed.

"Yes, ma'am."

"Huh. I guess I was so enthralled with the truck the first time I was in here that I overlooked it." Placing a hand on the truck, she continued. "I can't tell you how thrilled I was when I first saw this. It's going to be perfect for the Christmas tree farm."

He felt his brow shoot up. "Christmas tree farm?"

"You sound surprised. Why else would someone plant all those Christmas trees?"

Forcing himself not to be distracted he said, "I think the bigger question is why would they plant them on my family's property?"

"And you just expect me to believe you, a stranger."

He moved to the utility vehicle, pleased to see the key in the ignition. He rolled up the bay door. "Let's see if we can get this baby started." He eased onto the seat, set his foot on the brake and turned the key. The machine started immediately.

Noting that the noise seemed to be agitating her daughter, he promptly backed the UTV out of the garage.

"Care to drive?" He eyed Annalise as she approached.

"I'll hold off for now. Besides, you know where we're going."

Once she was buckled in with the little one in her lap, he eased the vehicle onto one of the narrow sandy roads that separated the rows of overgrown trees and proceeded cautiously, not wanting to upset Olivia. While a roof blocked the sun, the breeze moving over the half windshield tossed Annalise's and Olivia's hair.

He eyed the baby to see if she was bothered at all, but to his surprise, she seemed to be enjoying herself.

A short time later, they reached what had once been the farthest corner of Gary's property.

Hawkins stopped the vehicle. "See how this fence stretches straight across here, to the left and right?"

Annalise nodded.

Yet as he continued to drive, pointing out where the boundary lines should be versus where they were, he could see her eyes glazing over.

"I think the expression *Can't see the forest for the trees* is appropriate here," she finally said. "Because from where I sit, it looks like everything you're showing me is within my fence line."

He ignored the annoyance building inside of him. "That's because somebody moved the fence, removing what had been in place for decades." He eased his white-knuckle grip on the steering wheel. "Bottom line is that approximately three acres of the land these trees are on was taken from Prescott Farms."

Staring at him, she slowly shook her head. "Sorry, but unless you've got some concrete proof that I can actually see, I'm not buying it."

He drew in a long, slow breath. So she was ready to play hardball.

Well, so was he. This land belonged to him and his family.

"In that case, I'll have a copy of the survey by tomorrow afternoon. So I'd recommend you start making plans to have that fence returned to its proper position."

Chapter Two

Despite their invigorating ride through the Christmas trees, learning she owned a utility vehicle that would, indeed, come in handy, and staying up late to unpack as many boxes as possible, Annalise had still tossed and turned all night. While a part of her was annoyed by Hawkins' accusations that Uncle Gary had stolen a portion of Prescott land, she couldn't help wondering if, perhaps, it might be true. After all, it wasn't like she really knew her husband's uncle. She'd only spoken with him a couple of times, one of them being her and Dylan's wedding almost four years ago.

Yet no matter how sweet she found Uncle Gary's desire to make his wife's dream come true with the Christmas tree farm, something kept nagging at her, like a thorn you could feel but couldn't see.

What if, in his efforts to please his wife, he'd gotten carried away? Wanted more and more, the way Dylan always had? Would that drive Gary to steal land from the Prescotts?

A shudder ran through her. It all sounded like something out of the Old West. Stealing land. Though, she supposed it was better than cattle rustling. Or not.

What would she do if he had stolen the land? If the Prescotts were determined to reclaim it, Annalise would lose a good portion of her trees. Ones that wouldn't be ready to harvest for another couple of years. If she lost them, her inventory down the line would be severely lacking.

Now, as Olivia woke up from her nap Wednesday afternoon, panic welled within Annalise. There had to be some other option. Something she could do.

She moved across the wooden floor in the hallway to her daughter's bedroom and pushed open the door. "How's my little sweet pea?"

Smiling, Olivia held on to the side of her crib and bounced. Though the house was fully furnished, Annalise had still brought a few things of her own. Like the furniture from her daughter's room, as well as her queen-size bed and a few more items that would've been too much for her to lift alone. Hiring movers had been worth the extra expense, though. Not only had they done all of the heavy lifting but they'd also assembled things like the crib.

She scooped the child into her arms and blew raspberries on her tummy, producing the most intoxicating giggles.

"Somebody had a good nap." Too bad it wasn't Annalise.

She set to work changing Olivia's diaper, her mind quickly shifting back to the Christmas trees and Hawkins. Perhaps she could talk him into some sort of deal that would allow her to keep those three acres. Like renting the land.

But how much would that cost? Since the tree farm wasn't producing any income yet, she might not be able to afford that for a few years.

She set a refreshed Olivia on the floor. "Are you ready for a snack?"

"Ookee." The child babbled as she wandered barefoot into the hallway, continuing toward the country kitchen with white-painted cabinets, speckled gray countertops and two large windows over the vintage farmhouse sink that offered a view of the charming old barn.

"How about some apples with peanut butter?" They'd driven into Brenham after Hawkins left yesterday, to stock up on all of their favorite things.

"Ap. Ap." Olivia toddled into the kitchen.

After settling her daughter in her high chair, Annalise peeled and cut up the apple and spooned a small amount of peanut butter into a bowl. She set it on Olivia's tray before dropping into the wooden chair beside her.

Maybe Hawkins would consider a partnership of sorts. *And give him a say in how you run things?*

Her entire being cringed. No way. She didn't even know the man. All these years she *thought* she knew her husband and yet he'd constantly hidden things from her, telling her not to worry, that it was his job to take care of her and Olivia. It was only after his sudden death that Annalise learned how deeply in debt they were. His car and the house notes were enough to choke a horse. She'd had to use most of his life-insurance money to pay off a scary amount of credit card debt—which she'd known nothing about. The only good news was that property values had increased considerably since they'd purchased their home three years ago, so a bidding war had garnered her much more than she'd anticipated.

Still, the entire mess had taught her a hard lesson. Never again would she grant someone so much control over her life.

She nabbed a piece of Olivia's apple, knowing full well

that she was going to need some help with the tree farm. There was a lot of cleanup and trimming that needed to be done before opening day in late November. Something she'd never be able to tackle on her own.

A knock sounded at the front door, sending a wave of panic through Annalise.

It had to be Hawkins.

Forcing a calm she didn't feel, she moved into the living room. *Lord, did I misunderstand You? I thought for sure You were leading me to build a new life here at the farm. Now my plans are in jeopardy.*

Warm air spilled inside when she opened the door. As expected, Hawkins stood on her porch, a roll of papers in his hand.

"I wondered when we were going to see you." She peered up at him.

"I had some stuff to take care of at the ranch. However, I do have the proof that you requested."

"Great." She couldn't help the sarcasm in her tone. But then, what did he expect? He was pulling her dream, all her plans, right out from underneath her. Or a part of them, anyway.

Pushing the screen open, she waited for him to enter, then closed the door and motioned for him to follow her into the kitchen.

"Ookee," Olivia said when she spotted Hawkins.

"Seriously?" He twisted his ball cap backward, then knelt beside her high chair. "Are you always going to equate me with cookies?"

She held up a piece of apple. "Ap."

"Apples are yummy," he said. Then he was actually brave enough to eat the bite her daughter offered him. "Mmm. Delicious."

Olivia giggled.

The scene tugged at Annalise's heart. In the four months they'd had Olivia prior to Dylan's death, he hadn't paid her much attention. While Annalise tried to chalk it up to him being intimidated by a newborn, in her heart she knew both she and her daughter took second place in his life. It was Dylan's work that consumed him. Seemed whatever he did, he'd always wanted more. Making her wonder, if he had lived, how long would it have been before he was ready to replace Annalise?

Standing again, Hawkins faced her, the roll of papers still in his hand. "May I?" He motioned to the table which she'd managed to clear off while Olivia napped, save for one empty box.

She moved it to the floor, reluctantly nodding her agreement.

He spread out a series of documents and maps. "Okay, this is the survey of each of our properties." Yet while he pointed out a few landmarks on both his property and hers, the whole thing was foreign to her.

Shaking her head, she said, "I'm sorry, but I have no idea what's what on this."

"I anticipated as much, so I was able to print off a satellite image and overlay the survey so you could get a better understanding. That's what took me so long."

She couldn't have heard him correctly. He took extra steps to do something so she could better understand?

Call her weird, but that statement had her toes curling. Her parents, her husband, they all would've just told her either not to worry or to trust them. Yet Hawkins had gone the extra mile to lay things out so she could grasp what he was explaining to her.

"I know you're disappointed," he continued, "but as you can see here—" he pointed to the outline on the satellite image where she could clearly see all of the Christmas trees "—this is where the Prescott Farms property line actually exists."

While she appreciated his efforts to help her comprehend things, the reality of the situation had her feeling as though she might be sick. She'd worked so hard to learn about growing Christmas trees and running a business. Come up with so many plans for the farm's future.

"You're right. My trees are on your property. And while I have no idea why my husband's uncle would do such a thing—as far as I'm concerned, there's no excuse for stealing—I am willing to take responsibility. But I'm going to be honest with you." She dared to meet his gaze. "I was counting on those trees for income two or three years from now. So I'd like to make you an offer."

With one hand resting on the table as he leaned over the papers, he looked at her, a slight air of defiance simmering in his dark eyes. As though he was digging his heels in, ready to shoot down whatever she proposed. But at this point, what did she have to lose? If he said no, she'd have to regroup and determine how to make up for the loss. She had to try, though.

"What if we collaborated?"

Confusion creased his brow. "In what way?"

"If you agree to help me, I'll give you a third of all the sales from the Christmas tree farm. At least for this year. And then we'll see how things go."

He straightened, the muscle in his jaw pulsing beneath his scruff. "What sort of help?"

"No one has tended the trees or the area around them for several months. The grounds need to be mowed. Trees need trimming and shearing. And then there will be the grunt work of getting everything set up for sales."

"Annalise, I—"

She held up a hand to cut him off. "I'm not asking you

to do anything I won't be doing right alongside you. I was planning to hire someone—or several someones—to help, anyway. But I could give you a third of the profits instead."

"I hear what you're saying, but it's not just me you're dealing with."

"What do you mean?"

"My mom and sister. We're equal owners of Prescott Farms. So it's not just me who would have to agree, they'd have to, as well."

"Okay, then, I'll ask them, too."

"You should probably leave that to me."

And let him sway things for his benefit? Pass her Christmas tree farm off as foolishness the way her parents had?

"Besides, my sister is on her honeymoon."

Annalise lifted her chin. "When does she get back?"

"Friday night."

"Great, that'll give me a few days to pull together all of the ideas I want to present to them." And even if they said no, she would move forward with her plans because this was her home, her dream and her daughter's legacy. No matter how foolish people thought Annalise was, she would move forward with her plans and open the Christmas tree farm the day after Thanksgiving.

Hawkins was doing it again. Falling into the same old trap. Annalise had a problem. One he had the power to fix. And a part of him was ready to rush right in and do just that, the same way he'd done with Bridget. But just because he could didn't mean he should.

The look of devastation on Annalise's face when he'd provided the proof she'd requested had kept him awake half the night. Which only served to annoy him even more. He didn't want to feel bad for her. So it appeared she needed help. That she was in over her head. Bridget had always put on a pretty good show, too. His stomach still knotted whenever he thought about the sob stories she'd fed him. And he'd fallen for them, hook, line and sinker.

He wasn't about to let that happen again. Ever.

A handful of clouds drifted aimlessly across an otherwise-blue sky just after eleven Thursday morning as he maneuvered the Prescott Farms' utility vehicle across one of the many pastures covering their two-thousand acres. He eyed the cattle, doing his best to account for the entire herd, the way he'd done years ago. And while he wasn't as familiar with every cow and bull the way he'd been back then, his instincts still served him well, letting him know if something was amiss.

Too bad he didn't have those same instincts when it came to women.

He paused atop a ridge and looked out over the rolling hills of the Grand pasture. Why was he even entertaining Annalise's idea of a collaboration?

Because you're a chump.

Apparently.

He lowered the brim of his ball cap a notch. Perhaps it was time to tell his mother what ol' Gary had done. And while Hawkins would take care not to paint Annalise in a bad light, since she was just as much a victim in this as they were, he could probably count on his mother to shut down any talk of a collaboration without ever having to mention it to his sister.

Removing the phone from the clip on his belt, he dialed his mother.

"Good morning." As always, there was a smile in her voice.

"What are you up to today?"

"I'm just heating up some lunch for Bill and myself. Care to join us? I've got plenty of leftover pot roast."

Sounded a lot better than the ham sandwich he'd be making back at the cabin. "I'll be right over."

He ended the call, turned the utility vehicle around and made his way back to the cabin where he and his father had spent many a hunting or fishing weekend when Hawkins was growing up. For the last few years, though, his sister's husband and daughter had lived there, but now that Gloriana and Justin were married, they'd be taking over the house Hawkins and Gloriana had grown up in. The one his mother had lived in until she remarried this past May. Her new husband, Bill Krenek, had his own ranch, though, so it made more sense for her to move there than the other way around.

After swapping the utility vehicle for his pickup, he drove north of Hope Crossing proper, past cattle-dotted pastures and hayfields, arriving at Bill's place as the man was getting into his truck.

Hawkins lowered his window and rested his elbow atop the door. "Hope you're not leaving on my account."

"Naw. I got a cow that's havin' a tough time calving, so I need to keep an eye on her. You enjoy lunch with your mama, though."

"Will do." He waved as Bill pulled away, then parked in the same spot in front of the detached garage before making his way to the 1970s rambling brick ranch house that had been updated with a coat of light gray paint and black shutters.

Mom was waiting outside the door with a smile. "How's my baby boy today?"

He glowered. "Mom, I'm almost forty."

She waved a hand, then leaned in for a hug when he drew closer. "Doesn't matter. You're still my baby boy."

He slipped an arm around her shoulders, dwarfing her petite frame. "Whatever."

"Come on—" she motioned for him to follow "—let's get you some lunch."

"You don't need to tell me twice. I'm starving."

He followed her into the recently updated kitchen. The sleek white cabinets were quite a contrast to her country-style kitchen at Prescott Farms. "How are things going with Kyleigh?" His fifteen-year-old niece was staying with them while Justin and Gloriana were on their honeymoon in Colorado.

"She certainly has livened things up around here. It's gonna be kind of boring when she leaves." Mom paused beside the counter. "Would you like a sandwich or meat and potatoes?"

"Meat and potatoes, please." He'd had enough sandwiches this week. One of these days he'd need to go to a real grocery store instead of relying on Plowman's so he could have something more than deli meat and cheese slices in his refrigerator.

"So what's going on?" His mother piled roast beef and red potatoes onto a plate.

Good question. One he wasn't sure how to answer. Yet as Mom set his plate in the microwave and punched a few buttons, he decided he may as well tell her the whole story.

"I heard Gary Winston passed away."

Mom clutched one hand in the other and nodded. "Died of a broken heart, near as I can tell. He loved Eileen so much. Once she passed, I had a feeling it was only a matter of time. Those two were practically joined at the hip."

The microwave beeped, signaling Hawkins' lunch was ready.

"Grab you a chair," Mom said.

He snagged the wood chair nearest the window. The same one, he realized, that had been in her kitchen at Prescott Farms.

Moments later, she set the steaming plate in front of him, along with utensils and a napkin.

He breathed in the comforting aroma that brought back memories of his childhood.

Gathering a fork in one hand and a knife in the other, he smiled as she settled beside him. After a quick prayer, he allowed himself the pleasure of a large bite before continuing their conversation.

"I drove the fence lines of Prescott Farms Monday morning."

"That must've taken a while."

"Yes, but it's been a long time, and I wanted to make sure everything was as it should be."

She pushed out of her seat. "I presume it was." Peering over her shoulder, she retrieved a glass from the cupboard before moving to the refrigerator for ice and water.

"For the most part."

"Uh-oh." She set the glass in front of him before taking her seat again.

He rested his utensils on his plate and clasped his hands while he finished chewing. "I don't know when it happened, but it appears Gary moved his fence line, confiscating what I believe is about three acres of Prescott land."

Arms crossed atop the rustic table, she said, "That's not right. That's stealing."

"My thoughts exactly." The angst inside of him unraveled a notch. "So I went to confront him, unaware that he'd passed."

"And there was no one there." Mom shook her head. "I don't know what they're going to do with that place. He and Eileen had no children."

Picking up the knife and fork, he cut another chunk of beef. "No, but they had a nephew." He shoved the meat into his mouth.

His mother thought for a moment before wagging a finger through the air. "You know, now that you mention it, I remember meeting him *years* ago. He spent a couple of summers with them when he was about ten."

Though Hawkins hated to be so blunt, he said, "Yeah, well, he's dead, too." While he stabbed a piece of potato, his mother's eyes widened. "However, I met his widow the other day." He scarfed down the potato.

"How did you know who she was?"

Purposely leaving off the part about helping out Annalise at Plowman's on Monday, he said, "I went over there to confront Gary. Seems he left his land to his nephew and the nephew's heirs, which is comprised of a widow and their young child."

"How young?"

He reached for his glass, wondering why it mattered. "Maybe a year old." While he lifted a shoulder and took a drink, his mother gasped, pressing a hand against her chest.

Settling his cup on the table, he eyed the woman. "Did you know Gary and Eileen were planning to open a Christmas tree farm?"

She puffed out a laugh. "Are you kidding? They talked about nothing else for several years."

"Well, the niece-in-law picked up on that and is planning to fulfill their dream."

Again, Mom laid a palm to her chest, this time wearing a sad smile. "That is so sweet."

"No, it's not."

Her dark eyes, so much like his own, narrowed.

"A third of their trees are sitting on Prescott land."

She fell silent for a long moment, no doubt pondering the ramifications of Gary's preposterous move. "Yes, but it doesn't appear it's hurt us any."

His entire being cringed. From all appearances, he was going down in flames. Though, not without a fight.

Forgetting about his food, he said, "She wants to know if we'd be interested in a collaboration. If we will agree to help her trim the trees and get the place ready for business, she'll give us a third of whatever sales the tree farm makes."

Mom fell silent. Pondering. "Well. Sounds like a nice change of pace from cattle."

"They stole our land, Mom."

"From what you've said, just a couple of slivers. Corners at that. It's not like we lost a chunk of prime grazing land."

His core tightened. He thought for sure she'd be on his side. "But it's our land."

"And the niece said she'd pay us for the use of it."

Irritation had him pushing his plate away as his appetite faded. "She wants to meet with you, me and Gloriana."

His mother's smile nullified any hopes he had of shutting Annalise down. "I can see your sister being quite excited about this. Ever since she returned to Hope Crossing, she's been looking for ways to draw people to our little town. So when do we meet?"

Chapter Three

Still snuggled under the covers of her bed, Annalise opened her eyes Friday morning to discover the sun peering through the blinds. Rolling onto her side, she eyed the glowing numbers of the clock on her nightstand: 8:14!

She threw off the comforter to sit on the edge of the bed. She hadn't slept this late in ages. Shoving her hair out of her face, she glanced at the video monitor beside the clock. Olivia was still asleep. She must be worn out, too. Hadn't made a peep all night, as far as Annalise knew. All the stress of this week—traveling, getting their house set up, and all the back-and-forth with Hawkins— had obviously taken a toll on both of them.

Annalise stood and stretched, then changed into a pair of faded denim shorts and a deep green V-neck T-shirt, hoping to sneak in a cup of coffee before Olivia woke up. With so many things on her to-do list, she could use a few minutes of silence to collect her thoughts. There was so much she needed to tackle, most of it dealing with the Christmas trees in one form or another. Starting with clearing the overgrowth and shearing the trees. And she couldn't afford to waste time waiting on Hawkins.

Happy chatter echoed from the baby monitor, trumping her desires.

"I'm coming, sweet pea." After a quick dash into the en suite bathroom to run a brush through her hair, Annalise hurried into the hallway and made a left. A few short steps later, water splashed beneath her bare feet. Her gaze dropped to the wood floors and the water that not only covered them but continued to expand its reach throughout her house.

"Oh, no. No, no, no, no." Horror pummeled through her veins as she rushed into Olivia's room, splashing every step of the way. After gathering her daughter, she returned to her bedroom and grabbed her phone only to realize she had no idea who to call.

Where was all this water coming from?

Returning to the hall with Olivia on her hip, she stopped and listened. It sounded like it was coming from the secondary bathroom.

She hurried to the end of the hall. The space with powder-blue walls lay straight ahead while another hallway to her right led into the kitchen. A quick glance in that direction revealed the water had already made it there.

Continuing into the bathroom, she discovered water spilling from the tank at the back of the commode.

"Eww." Her entire being cringed at the knowledge she was walking through toilet water. In her bare feet, no less.

A second later, a sense of relief swept over her when she realized the tank held *clean* water. Now she just had to find a way to stop it.

She set Olivia on the commode lid and tried to turn off the valve near the wall, but it wouldn't budge. With an aggravated groan, she grabbed her daughter and rushed to the kitchen where she had a small toolbox. She located a pair of pliers before returning to the bathroom to try again, but the thing still wouldn't move.

Suddenly, an atrocious odor reached her nose. "Whoo. You a stinky baby, Olivia."

After a hasty diaper change in her bedroom, Annalise carried her daughter outside to look for the cutoff valve. In the city, they were usually at the curb, but she doubted that was the case out here in the country.

Baby affixed to her side, she circled the house multiple times, uncertain where it could be or what it might look like. Soon, Olivia was voicing her displeasure.

Realizing she was probably hungry, Annalise trekked back inside to the kitchen to get Olivia something to eat. Opening the refrigerator, she grabbed a yogurt pouch and the milk. After filling a sippy cup, she returned the milk to the fridge before snagging the cup and the bunch of bananas from the counter and hurried back outside to the porch. So much for her coffee.

After setting Olivia in one of the wicker chairs and plying her with the yogurt, Annalise pulled her phone from her pocket. She had to call someone, but who? Her insurance company? Plumber? Remediation company?

She decided to start with her insurance company and was on hold when she spotted Hawkins' truck coming up the drive.

A groan escaped her lips. She did not want to deal with him right now. Not while she was in the midst of a crisis.

Phone still pressed to her ear, she stood and moved to the wooden railing as he got out of his truck. "Sorry, this isn't a good time."

He continued toward her, his expression unreadable. "Then, at least give me your phone number so I don't have to drive a mile and half around the horn just to pass along information."

Information? "Sure. It's—"

A voice came through the telephone line. "*We are currently experiencing a higher-than-normal call volume. Please leave your name, phone number and policy number, and a representative will call you back.*"

She slumped against the railing. At the moment, she wasn't even sure where to find her policy number.

Tears pricked her eyes as she ended the call. Willing them away, she faced Hawkins. "Do you have any idea where I might find the water cutoff to the house?"

One dark brow lifted. "Is there a problem?"

Frustration finally got the best of her. "My house is flooding." Her voice quivered. "The toilet tank is overflowing, the cutoff valve won't budge, and I can't find the main to turn off water to the house."

He took the steps in a single leap and tugged open the screen door. "Which way to the bathroom?"

"Down the hall to the left." She grabbed Olivia and followed, only to see him reverse course when his attempt to move the valve failed.

"Your main should be in the pump house." He tossed the words over his shoulder as he moved outside again.

She followed, the screen door smacking shut behind her as he bounded off the porch.

"Pump house?" Her short legs coupled with Olivia's added weight made it difficult to keep up with Hawkins' long strides.

"Yeah. Where the cutoff is." He continued around the house, scanning the backyard before heading to the garage where the utility vehicle and truck were parked.

"I thought this was a garage." She followed him inside as he moved behind the door where a blue tank with pipes going into or coming out of it was tucked in the corner.

Reaching down, he twisted a black lever before addressing her again. "This is the air tank." He pointed. "It creates the pressure for the pump to get the water from the well to the house. So we call this—" he swept a hand through the air, motioning to the rest of the garage "—a pump house."

She could feel her cheeks heating. "I don't know why you referred to it as a garage, then, but that's good to know. Thank you. I've never dealt with a pump before."

Hands slung low on his hips, he stared down at her. "Obviously."

Between his six-foot-something frame plus at least another inch of cowboy boots and her in bare feet, she suddenly felt incredibly small.

"Guess I'd better start working to get that water out of my house." With Olivia still on her hip, Annalise spotted a broom hanging on the wall and grabbed it on her way out.

As they stepped under the shade of the oak tree on the side of the house, Hawkins said, "You'll need to contact your insurance company." He must think she didn't have a brain in her head.

"That's what I was *trying* to do when you showed up, but they put me on terminal hold, then wanted to call me back, but I didn't have my policy number." Her voice cracked.

Olivia began to whimper.

Hawkins stepped in front of them, stopping her advance. His dark gaze bore into her for the longest time before he reached for the broom. "Find yourself a seat somewhere and catch your breath while I assess the damage." Obviously he thought her as incapable as her parents and Dylan had.

She tightened her grip on the broom. "I can—"

"I know, but you look like you could use a moment to

gather your thoughts. Maybe try your insurance company again." He smiled at Olivia. "And this little one needs to know her mama is all right." The compassion in his expression was unexpected.

Nodding, she released her hold on the broom, and an hour later was still in one of the porch chairs, Olivia in her lap while Annalise wound down the call with her insurance company, when another truck pulled into her drive. A short time later, she watched as a man and woman emerged and promptly began retrieving items from the truck's bed. A shop vac, a fan.

"The remediation company should be getting in contact with you shortly, Mrs. Grant."

Annalise had almost forgotten she was on hold. "Wonderful, thank you so much." She was tucking her phone away when Hawkins joined her on the porch.

He eyed the couple as they approached. "Y'all made good time."

"When there's water involved, there's no time to waste," said the blonde who looked to be in her mid-sixties, with dark eyes reminiscent of Hawkins'.

He looked at Annalise. "This is my mother, Francie Prescott—uh, make that Krenek—and her husband, Bill." He eyed the man wearing a well-worn cowboy hat. "This is Annalise…" Glancing her way, he said, "Sorry, I don't know your last name."

"Grant." She stepped forward, feeling rather uneasy. After all, she owned the trees that were unlawfully on Prescott land. "It's nice to meet you. Sorry about the circumstances, though."

Francie continued onto the porch, carrying a box fan. "Don't you worry. Neighbors may not be as near out here in the country, but we always look after each other." Setting the fan on the wood-plank floor, she smiled at Olivia. "And who is this little dumpling?"

"This is my daughter, Olivia."

As if realizing she was the center of attention, the child grinned and practically threw herself toward Francie.

The woman laughed as she caught her. "Aren't you the cutest thing?" She smoothed a hand over Olivia's downy hair. "I'd love to play with you, sweetheart, but I need to help your mama with all this water."

"Ba?" Olivia clapped.

"No, no bathing in this water, darlin'."

"Here's that ball float you asked for." Bill handed Hawkins a plastic bag containing a black ball.

"What is that?" Annalise asked as Francie passed Olivia back to her.

"It's what keeps your toilet tank from overflowing," said Hawkins. "The one in your tank is broken."

"So it's an easy fix?"

Both Hawkins and Bill nodded.

"That's a relief." Still, as Annalise watched Bill and Francie follow Hawkins into her house, her insides tangled. While she was grateful for their help, she was pretty sure the fate of the trees on Prescott land had just been sealed. Hawkins and his mother probably saw her as the same inept woman everyone else always had. She hadn't even known about the pump.

She hugged Olivia, well aware that the Prescotts would never want to work with her now. Annalise would simply have to find a way to make the Christmas tree farm work without their land or any collaboration.

Hawkins closed his laptop on the kitchen table in his father's old hunting cabin after lunch Saturday, annoyed with himself for researching Christmas tree farming in

Texas. Dragging a hand through his hair, he let go a sigh. He was getting drawn into Annalise's world a little more every day. Just the way he had with Bridget. And he was the one who had come out looking like a chump. Falling for her lies, allowing her to manipulate him.

Even now, memories of the way she'd made him believe her mother needed money for her medical expenses or that Bridget had needed to visit the woman in Florida stirred his ire. By the time he'd learned that her mother was alive and well on one of Alaska's remote islands, he was out thousands of dollars. Though, not everything Bridget said had been a lie. She had, indeed, traveled to Florida. With some other guy.

Annalise didn't ask for your help. You offered.

Yeah, well, that's how things had started with Bridget, too. Give them and inch and…

Still, he needed to convince his mother and sister that a collaboration with Annalise was a bad idea before it was too late. Because if things went crossways, he wouldn't be the only one paying the price this time.

A knock sounded at the door.

He stood and moved across the longleaf-pine floor from the kitchen into the adjoining living room and yanked it open.

His sister stood there, her dark hair pulled back in a ponytail while she grinned from ear to ear. The sparkle in her hazel eyes was hard to miss, and it did his heart good to see her so happy. Her life had changed considerably over the past several months. She'd gone from being a career-driven workaholic who hadn't darkened the door of a church since their parents made her attend in high school to a God-fearing woman devoted to her family and bent on letting the whole world know that small towns had a lot to offer.

One look at him, though, and her smile faltered. "What's got you in such a foul mood?" She brushed past him.

"Hello to you, too." He glanced outside. "Where's Mom?"

"She'll be here shortly." While he closed the door, she continued. "So what's this I hear about a Christmas tree farm? I can't wait to see it. We could use something like that around here. Something that would lure people to Hope Crossing at other times of the year, not just in June for the rodeo."

Obviously his mother had already talked with her. "Doesn't it bother you that our land was stolen?"

"Not when I think of all the possibilities. I mean, if we'd discovered early on that the fence had been moved, I probably would've been upset, but now that we're looking at another source of income…"

"Like it would bring in very much."

"Big brother, you have no idea. Done well, places like that can be a real draw. An event." She let out a giddy little squeal. "I can't wait to see it. Can we go now? I mean, after Mom gets here."

"Wouldn't you rather sit down and tell me about your honeymoon or something?"

"It was Colorado. Gorgeous scenery, including lots of fall color, and *much* cooler temperatures. Throw in my handsome husband, and it was five days of pure perfection."

There was another knock at the door before Mom poked her head inside.

"Oh, good, you're here." Gloriana looked at Hawkins as their mother joined them. "We're ready when you are."

He held up his hands. "Don't you think we should discuss this first? I mean, we don't even know Annalise. She could be blowing smoke for all we know."

"True." Gloriana nodded. "But how are we supposed

to make an informed decision if we don't have all the facts?"

"Annalise seems like a lovely young woman," his mother added. "I mean, she was under a *lot* of stress yesterday, and yet she was so very gracious. I suppose, if anything, I'm concerned that running a business might be too much for her while Olivia is so little."

Finally, something he could latch on to. "That's a good point, Mom. Toddlers require a lot of attention."

"Though, now that I think about it," she continued, "Kyleigh would make a wonderful babysitter."

Kyleigh was Justin's fifteen-year-old adopted daughter, and Gloriana was her birth mother. Something they'd only discovered this past spring, after Justin and Gloriana fell in love. Yet while Hawkins was still getting to know his niece, he had a feeling she'd embrace babysitting with the same gusto she approached everything else.

"She's actually been wanting to do more babysitting," said Gloriana. "She's sat for my friend Tori's little boy a couple of times and, according to Tori, Aiden adores her."

Both women stared up at him.

Mom smiled. "Is Annalise expecting us?"

He retrieved his phone from his pocket. "Let me give her a call."

Naturally, she answered on the first ring and was waiting on the porch when they arrived a short time later. After his mother and sister had sufficiently fussed over Olivia, they all moved to the garage where the utility vehicle was parked. Though, they were sidetracked when Gloriana spotted the red pickup.

"This is the quintessential Christmas tree truck." She looked at Annalise. "I hope you plan to use this as part of your display."

"Absolutely. It exudes that whole Christmas vibe, so it'll definitely take center stage somewhere."

While the women slid onto the bench seat of the UTV, he folded himself into its bed. Not something he would normally do, but it was either that or walk. Besides, with the baby in the front, he was certain Annalise would be taking things slowly.

She showed them two different types of trees, Virginia pines and Leyland cypresses. They grew in separate areas, and there were far more pines. According to Annalise, the cypress trees were perfect for people with allergies.

When they returned forty minutes later, Gloriana wasted no time surveying their surroundings. "What a great old barn." Under the shade of the oak tree, she peered across the drive. "With that weathered wood and rusted metal roof, it feeds into the whole ambience of this place. Inviting. Cozy. Timeworn tradition."

Hawkins watched Annalise standing between his mother and sister, her daughter in her arms and a glimmer of excitement in her eyes.

"I agree." She looked at each of the women. "If you'd like to come inside, I can show you the journals Gary and Eileen kept with all of their ideas, as well as some of my own thoughts."

"Yes, definitely." Gloriana had a similar spark in her eyes. And while it could be residual from her honeymoon, Hawkins suspected she was every bit as excited about this tree farm as Annalise. And that didn't bode well for him.

Inside the farmhouse, the living-room furniture sat atop risers, and the sound of air movers left by the remediation company had him wondering how she expected them to carry on any sort of reasonable conversation.

But she promptly moved about the space, turning them off until silence reigned.

Setting her daughter on the floor that no longer showed any sign of moisture, Annalise said, "If you'd like to join me in the kitchen, I baked some cookies earlier."

"You don't have to tell me twice." Mom hurried after her while Hawkins remained near the front door.

Gloriana moved beside him and leaned his way. "I can't begin to tell you how much potential this place has." With that, she followed the other women into the kitchen.

Across the room, near the large opening between the living room and kitchen, Olivia looked from the women to him as if trying to decide which way to go. She sure was a cutie.

He smiled. "Whatcha think, little one?"

She giggled and began toddling toward him, picking up speed with each and every step until he feared the momentum was going to send her tumbling head over heels. Sure enough, a moment later, she stumbled.

With a single step, he closed the distance between them, leaned forward and caught her. He straightened, adjusting her in his arms. "That was a close one."

Her blue eyes captured his, and she began jabbering as though nothing had happened.

Of course, he couldn't understand a word, so he simply smiled and said, "Is that so?"

"Hawk, if you want a cookie, you'd better get in here before I eat them all."

"That's my sister, Gloriana," he whispered to Olivia as he moved toward the kitchen. "She can be a little bossy sometimes."

"Ookee."

"Oh, you heard that part, huh?"

When he walked into the kitchen, three pairs of eyes stared at him.

"What?"

The women exchanged looks then Annalise held out a plate. "Cookie?"

Once Annalise had settled her daughter into her high chair with her own cookie, she grabbed a small stack of leather-bound journals, a thick spiral notebook and a three-ring binder from an antique sideboard along the wall and placed them on the table before taking a seat opposite him. Then slowly and methodically, she went over all of Gary and Eileen's plans, along with her own ideas not just for this year but for the extended future. Plans that included hayrides and a petting zoo, as well as thoughts on prolonging the season to include a pumpkin patch in the fall. Even talk of a plant nursery, though that was a ways down the road.

His mother and sister were visibly impressed, and he couldn't disagree.

"You've put a lot of thought into this," he said.

"Since visiting here two months ago I've thought about little else." She picked up her daughter, who had long since been freed from the confines of her chair and had been entertaining herself with some toys Annalise brought into the kitchen. "As far as I'm concerned, this farm is Olivia's future, so I want to see it succeed."

Without looking away, he said, "And our land?"

She lifted a shoulder as Olivia squirmed her way back to the floor. "I don't see why we couldn't work together. We could give it a try this year and see how things go."

"I've got to admit," said Gloriana, "I have a *ton* of ideas rolling through my head. How to promote it, activities. And you're right about carrying those items that go hand-in-hand with the trees. Stands, fresh wreaths and garlands."

"When I was a little girl," Mom began, "we used to make our own wreaths and garlands all the time."

Beside him, Gloriana cast their mother a slightly irritated glance. "How come we never did that?"

Mom shrugged. "Probably because you wouldn't sit still long enough."

"I can believe that." The comment earned him a swat from his sister.

Despite his misgivings, he found their excitement contagious. He could see people making the drive out here for some good old-fashioned holiday fun. But he was still leery of Annalise.

Eying her across the table, he said, "Of course, we'll have to have our attorney draw up a formal agreement." He had to ensure his family and their land were protected.

To her credit, she never flinched. "I understand."

"Well, then—" Gloriana looked around the table "—it looks like the Prescotts are going into the Christmas tree business."

And Hawkins planned to be there every step of the way to make sure they weren't taken advantage of.

Chapter Four

Wearing her favorite dress—a pale pink, short-sleeved cotton number adorned with tiny sunflowers—Annalise approached the steepled, beige-brick church with Olivia in her arms the next morning, apprehension nipping at the heels of her matching strappy sandals. Even before leaving Dallas, she knew finding a church home would be a priority when she arrived in Hope Crossing, though that didn't make the act of walking into a group of strangers any easier. Even if they were fellow believers. All eyes were sure to be upon her, and that always made her uneasy.

As the clouds dissipated and the sun emerged, Annalise decided it couldn't be any worse than facing the entire Prescott family, embarrassingly aware that a third of her tree farm was sitting unlawfully on their land. Yet while Hawkins was intimidating at times, his mother and sister had made her want to put on a pot of coffee and sit down for a long chat so she could get to know them better.

Nearing the dark-wood and stained-glass doors, she took a deep breath. Her new church home was where she and Olivia would build friendships, so she prayed God would lead her to the place He had for her.

Cool air rushed over her as she stepped inside the tiled foyer. Two older men she assumed were ushers promptly greeted her, and after learning she was new, the taller of the two, Willard, escorted her and Olivia down a hallway to their left, nodding to a couple of other parishioners as they passed, all the while sharing basic information about the church, most of which she'd already found online.

Soon they stopped outside of a Noah's Ark themed room where a petite woman with short, silver hair watched a little boy who looked to be about three push a fire truck over a colorful animal-adorned rug.

"Dottie," Willard called.

The woman turned, her smile bright as she approached the half door. Beaming at Olivia, she clasped her hands together. "Oh, aren't you just too cute for words!"

"This here's Annalise and her daughter, Olivia." Willard looked from the woman to Annalise. "Dottie's my wife."

She shifted her blue eyes to Annalise. "Is this your first time joining us?"

"Yes, ma'am. I just moved to Hope Crossing."

"Well, we are delighted to have you." Her focus again moved to Olivia. "And don't you worry about this little darlin', hon. I've been takin' care of babies since before you were born. Miss Olivia here may fuss a bit when you leave, being here for the first time and all, but I guarantee I'll have her settled in no time."

Annalise appreciated the reassurance. Though, given the way Olivia readily went to Dottie, much the way she had with Francie on Friday, Annalise doubted there'd be any fussing. At least, she hoped not.

She handed off the diaper bag and said goodbye to Olivia, her insides knotting as Willard led her back to the sanctuary.

"I think you'll find folks here at Hope Crossing Bible Church welcoming." The man obviously sensed her unease. He paused in the center aisle midway between the altar and the back of the sanctuary that boasted beautiful stained-glass windows and rested a hand on the back of one of the cushioned wood pews. "We're all sinners in need of a Savior."

Annalise couldn't help smiling. "I agree completely."

"Annalise?"

Turning, she saw Francie approach with Bill at her side, sans the cowboy hat, revealing light brown hair with a touch of gray.

The sight of a familiar face eased Annalise's anxiety. "Good morning."

The older woman wrapped her in a hug as though she'd known Annalise all her life. "I'm delighted you're here." Releasing her, she took a step back. "Though, I'm disappointed in myself for not inviting you when we were at your place yesterday."

"That's all right. I—"

"Annalise, you're here." Gloriana greeted her with a smile and a hug that erased any remaining nervousness.

"I am."

Taking a step back, Gloriana gestured to the man and teenage girl beside her. "This is my husband, Justin, and my daughter, Kyleigh." She turned her attention to them. "This is Annalise, the one who has the Christmas tree farm."

Her husband's smile reached his blue-green eyes as he held out his hand. "Nice to meet you." As she took hold, he added, "I've heard quite a bit about you since my wife returned from your place yesterday."

"Oh?" She released his hand, her gut tightening as

her gaze darted between him and his wife. What all had Gloriana said?

"She and Ky are beside themselves over the Christmas tree farm," he added.

"And you have a baby." Kyleigh bounced on the balls of her wedged sandals.

"Is this a family meeting I wasn't invited to?"

They turned in unison as Hawkins approached. And when he spotted Annalise, his smile all but evaporated.

"We're just welcoming Annalise," said Francie.

Gloriana elbowed her mother. "Mom, are you thinking what I'm thinking?"

Francie winked. "I believe so." She turned her attention to Annalise. "Would you and Olivia like to join us after church for Sunday dinner?"

Annalise saw Hawkins frown. While he'd helped her countless times this past week, he didn't seem near as excited about a collaboration on the Christmas tree farm as his mother and sister were, despite agreeing to the arrangement.

"Oh, I don't know. Olivia will probably be ready for nap by then, and no one wants to deal with a cranky baby."

"Nonsense." Francie waved a hand. "There will be plenty of us to keep her entertained."

"How old is she?" Kyleigh tucked her long, dark brown hair behind one ear.

"Sixteen months."

"Aww." The girl smiled. "I should get to know her. That way, if you ever need a babysitter…"

"Kyleigh makes an excellent point," said Gloriana. "Though, I wouldn't mind some baby snuggles, too."

As the piano began to play, Francie said, "Sounds like it's settled, then."

"We'd best grab a seat." Bill gestured to the pew they'd been blocking.

While Annalise was happy not to be sitting alone, being tucked between Kyleigh and Hawkins wasn't exactly ideal. Kyleigh was fine, but Hawkins' nearness only heightened her awareness of him. From the way his light blue button-down highlighted his deep brown eyes to his smooth baritone singing voice to his thick dark hair that'd been freed from the confines of the ball cap she was used to seeing. Then there was that perfectly groomed five-o'clock shadow that gave him a slightly dangerous look.

Stop thinking like that! You're in church.

Lassoing her wayward thoughts, she managed to concentrate on the rest of the pastor's sermon and found herself really enjoying his message. She liked his no-nonsense approach to preaching.

When the service was over, Francie caught up to Annalise in the aisle. "You're staying for Sunday school, I assume. Which class are you planning to attend?"

Annalise stared at the woman. "I guess I hadn't thought that far ahead. What are my options?"

Taking hold of her son's arm, Francie said, "You could go to the single-adult class with Hawkins."

He glowered at his mother, his brow puckering. "You know that class is nothing but a bunch of college-age kids."

His mother waved him off. "No, you're thinking of the young-singles class. This is a new one. Gabriel Vaughn teaches it. You remember him."

"Yeah, I do. He was a couple of years behind me in school."

"Tori's been going to it." Gloriana slid her purse over her shoulder. "And speaking of Tori…"

A cute blonde approached, her smile wide. After a

brief introduction and learning that Tori and Gloriana had been besties since grade school, Tori escorted Annalise to their small classroom. Something Annalise was more than a little grateful for. While she knew Francie meant well, Annalise would prefer not to spend any more time with Hawkins than necessary. Circumstances beyond their control had already forced them together way too many times this week. And while his interaction with Olivia never failed to melt Annalise's heart, she was growing weary of feeling indebted to him.

After class, she and Tori chatted all the way to the nursery. Since she was also widowed and a single mother, they had a lot in common and probably could've talked all afternoon, but Annalise didn't want to keep Francie waiting.

With her daughter in her arms, Annalise made her way to the front of the virtually empty building, while Tori went the opposite direction. Now that Annalise knew there was another parking lot closer to the nursery, she'd be sure to park in it next week.

She pushed through the stained-glass doors into the bright sunshine to find the parking lot empty except for her SUV and Hawkins' truck. And he was standing in front of it. Actually, he was leaning against the front bumper, arms crossed, looking slightly perturbed.

Approaching, she eyed him. "Problem?"

"Just waiting on you."

"Why?"

"So you can follow me to my mom's place."

Squinting against the sun, she said, "She gave me her address."

He pushed off the truck and took a step in her direction. "And I'm sure your GPS would take you there without issue. However, my mother is old-school and insisted I lead you."

Annalise cringed. "I'm sorry. If I'd known you were waiting, I wouldn't have—"

A car horn had them both turning then waving to Tori as she pulled onto the road and sped away.

Returning her attention to Hawkins, Annalise said, "Let me get Olivia buckled into her seat, and we'll be on our way." She slid the backpack from her shoulder and fumbled for her keys.

"I can hold her." He reached for Olivia, his smile wide.

Ignoring the tug on her heart, Annalise located her keys, then looked up to discover her daughter tentatively exploring the scruff on Hawkins' chin with her hand.

"What do you think?" His gaze was fixed on the child. Her child. "Is it prickly?"

Olivia scrunched up her little face and giggled, patting her hands together.

"Oh, you think it's funny, huh?"

Annalise pressed the button on the fob to unlock her vehicle, needing a distraction from the sweet scene. "So are we going to Prescott Farms?" She opened the door and deposited the diaper bag and her purse inside before reaching for Olivia.

"No." Hawkins passed her daughter to her. "Bill's ranch is north of town. Mom moved there after they married in May. But Sunday dinner has always been her thing."

After buckling Olivia into her seat, Annalise closed the back door and moved to the driver's seat while Hawkins rounded his truck. She shoved the key in the ignition and turned it, but instead of starting right up, the engine groaned.

Her stomach knotted. After all of the things that had gone wrong this week—losing her wallet, the property issue with the trees and her house flooding—she didn't need any more problems. At least not in the presence of Hawkins Prescott.

She turned the key again, but the groan coming from beneath the hood only grew weaker.

Please, God. Haven't I been embarrassed enough this week?

A knock on her window made her jump.

She pressed the button to roll the window down, but nothing happened.

Squaring her shoulders, she pushed the door open and stepped outside again to face the man whose smile had disappeared.

"Sounds like your battery is on life support."

"Yep." She stared at the pavement. "Can't say I've heard it do that before."

"When was the last time you had it checked?"

She crossed her arms, refusing to look at him for fear of seeing the same you-should-have-known-better expression and headshake Dylan and her parents always seemed to offer. "I assume they do that whenever I have the oil changed, so a little over a week ago. Right before we moved here. They never mentioned anything about a problem, though."

His jaw twitched as he continued to watch her. "I'll get my jumper cables."

"What if it won't start?" she called after him.

Pausing, he rubbed the back of his neck. "We'll cross that bridge when we come to it."

Her entire being cringed as he continued to his truck. The last thing she wanted was for Hawkins to come to her rescue again. But with the way things had played out this week, she'd not only be surprised if her car started, she had a sneaking suspicion said bridge was likely to be washed out, too.

No wallet at Plowman's, then the water leak, and now her car wouldn't start. From where Hawkins stood, Annalise Grant appeared predisposed to disaster. Yet she'd packed up her baby girl and moved to the country, right next door to Prescott Farms. Even worse he'd agreed to work with her.

No, your mother and sister did.

He'd gone along with it, however, after being drawn in by all of her plans.

Now, head under the hood of her late-model SUV, he adjusted the jumper cables clamped to the battery terminals, wondering what on earth God was trying to teach him through all of this. Hawkins had no desire to come to the rescue of another woman. But since theirs were the only two cars in the parking lot, he supposed he didn't have much of a choice. He couldn't just leave Annalise here with her baby.

He stepped away from the engine and moved around the vehicle to the open driver's door.

"Give it another try," he hollered over the roar of his pickup's engine, then held his breath, praying the vehicle would start.

The engine attempted to turn over, only to die seconds later. No doubt about it, her battery was a goner.

He motioned for her to turn off the vehicle, then returned to the engine and removed the cables before doing the same at his truck.

She was beside him as he closed the truck's hood. "You should go on to your mother's. I can call roadside assistance."

Moving to the side of his truck, he opened the back door and tossed the cables inside. If they were in the city, that would be a logical option. And while they weren't quite in the middle of nowhere, the notion was still laughable.

He tossed the door closed before settling his hands on his hips. "First of all, roadside assistance isn't just up the road. Who knows how many hours it would take them to get to you? If they would at all. Second, do you really think I'm the kind of guy who'd leave you and Olivia out here alone with no food, no water and no air-conditioning?" He glanced at the sun that seemed to be growing hotter by the minute. "Besides, you've met my mother. She'd tan my hide if I did something like that."

The corners of Annalise's mouth twitched. "I doubt she'd tan your hide, though I could see Francie giving you a good tongue-lashing."

Wiping the sweat from his brow, he said, "You have no idea." He blew out a breath. "We need to get your battery replaced because, as a single mom, you don't need to be without transportation."

"And how do we do that when it won't start?"

"I'll have to remove the battery, drive to Brenham to get a replacement, then come back and install it."

Her shoulders sagged. "I hate to make you do that."

"Do you have another option?"

Her countenance fell. "No. I don't suppose I do. But what about your mother? She's expecting you."

"She's expecting you, too. So I'll remove the battery, then we'll take my truck to Mom's for lunch, and I'll run to Brenham afterward."

Her brow puckered above her sunglasses as she lifted her face to meet his. "You've already done so much for me. I hate the thought of having to put you out again. Especially when it's such a beautiful day. I don't want to take you away from your own plans."

"The only plans I have revolve around a football game, and that's not until tonight. However, I am starving, so you get Olivia and her seat moved to the truck while I tend to the battery so we can be on our way."

Both tasks were completed faster than he'd expected, and before he knew it, they were sitting in his mother's dining room, enjoying her famous chicken-fried steak with mashed potatoes and cream gravy.

"Everything is delicious, Francie." To his left, at the same oval dark walnut dining table he'd grown up with, Annalise held Olivia in her lap and fed her small spoonful of potatoes. "Thank you for inviting us."

"You're welcome, dear. It's my son's favorite meal, and since this is our first time to gather as a family since he returned from Alaska, I had to go all out."

He swiped a napkin across his mouth. "I think I'll hold off on dessert until I get back from Brenham." Leaning back in his seat, he patted his stomach. "I'm out of room."

"You assume there'll be some dessert left when you get back." Gloriana eyed him across the table. "Mom's coconut cream pie is both of our favorites."

"Yeah, but this is *my* meal, so hands off."

His sister narrowed her hazel eyes. "Mom said the meal was for you. She didn't say anything about dessert."

"All right, you two." At the end of the table, their mother glared at both of them. "You're behaving like children. Only part of the reason I made two pies."

From the opposite end of the table, beside Hawkins, Bill smirked as he looked from Hawkins to Gloriana and back. "And one of them's just for me."

"What?" Hawkins and Gloriana both balked.

"He's kidding," their mother quickly announced, sending her husband a scathing look. Setting her napkin beside her plate, she looked at Annalise. "Why don't you let Gloriana, Kyleigh and me watch Olivia while you go with Hawkins?"

As if sitting beside Annalise in church, her soft floral fragrance wafting around him, hadn't been enough torture. "Mom, that's not fair to Annalise. She might not be comfortable leaving her daughter. She can stay. I'll go."

Head cocked, Mom's dark gaze moved to their guest. "Annalise, what would you prefer?"

Hawkins frowned at his mother, his frustration mounting. He was going to have to have a talk with her about her not-so-subtle attempts to push him and Annalise together.

With one arm around Olivia, Annalise swapped the spoon for a napkin and wiped her daughter's mouth. "I would prefer *not* to impose on any of you. I mean, you've all helped me so much already. With the flood at my place, agreeing to collaborate on the tree farm." She glanced Hawkins' way. "From the moment I arrived in Hope Crossing, you Prescotts have done so much for me." She heaved a sigh. "I don't suppose there are any Ubers in Hope Crossing, are there?"

They all shook their heads.

Olivia began to whimper, rubbing her eyes.

Mom pushed her chair out to come alongside Annalise. Holding out her hands, she said, "May I?"

Before Annalise could respond, Olivia reached for his mother.

Taking the child in her arms, Mom returned to her seat. "It's all right, sweetheart." She patted Olivia's bottom. "Even the best of us get cranky when we're tired." She looked at Annalise. "It's up to you, dear, but Olivia will be perfectly fine here if you'd like to go with Hawkins."

"Though, she's apt to be a little spoiled by the time you get back." Gloriana winked.

After a moment, Annalise sent Hawkins a resigned look. "I guess we should be going, then."

They wasted no time getting into his truck, and the first few minutes of their trip passed by in silence, save for the country music playing low through the speakers. He focused on the road while Annalise took in the scenery. Something that suited him just fine. Until he noticed the uncharacteristic creases in her brow.

Both hands on the steering wheel, he did his best to ignore them, reminding himself of what she'd said at the table about not wanting to impose. But try as he might, the distress in her eyes still got to him.

"You don't like leaving Olivia, do you?"

She lifted a shoulder, her gaze never leaving the road. "I'm used to it. She was in day care when we lived in Dallas. And she will be again, once we're settled and I go back to work."

"What do you do?"

"I'm a financial analyst for a nonprofit organization that allows me to work remotely."

"A lot of us are doing that nowadays." Himself included, though he would have to make the occasional site visit.

Still sensing something had her upset, he said, "So what's bothering you?"

After a moment, she sighed and looked his way. "I don't want you and your family to feel like I'm taking advantage of you. Everything that could have possibly gone wrong this week did, and you ended up coming to my rescue each and every time."

He slowly maneuvered around a curve, wondering if she'd read his mind. "Okay, I'll admit that I was skeptical that day at Plowman's. The rest was just coincidence." And he always happened to be there.

While a smile tugged at her pretty pink lips, she said, "Don't get me wrong, I appreciate everything you all have done for me and Olivia." She stared at her tightly clasped hands in her lap. "It's just that people have always thought of me as incapable. Like I needed to be taken care of."

The admission had him glancing her way. "What people?"

"My parents. Husband." She again took in the pastures that whizzed past. "Dylan always told me not to worry. That it was his job to take care of his family. Then he died, and I soon discovered we'd been living *way* beyond our means."

She faced Hawkins. "The sad part is, I never wanted the flashy cars or the big house. I grew up with all of that. My parents were all about appearances. But all I've ever wanted was a simple life. One filled with love and laughter. Someone to hold my hand when times were tough." She crossed her arms over her chest. "Sometimes I wonder if Dylan ever really knew me at all."

Hawkins' grip tightened on the steering wheel. He hadn't expected all of that. A grieving widow, perhaps, but not an angry one. That is, assuming everything she said was true.

Clearing his throat, he cut her a glance. "How long has your husband been gone?"

"A year. Something called sudden cardiac death. Pretty strange for a guy who spent way too much time at the gym and appeared to be the picture of health."

Hawkins slowed his speed as they approached the Brenham city limits. "Olivia must've been pretty little."

Annalise nodded. "Four months old."

He shook his head. "That's rough." The kid would

never have any memories of her father. "Do you have any siblings?"

"No."

The truck rumbled over the railroad tracks.

"How did your parents feel about you moving so far away?"

"They weren't pleased." She cocked her head. "But then, it's not the first time they've disagreed with one of my decisions."

"Oh?"

"You'd have thought the world was coming to an end when I decided to take a job with a nonprofit instead of joining their company."

"What do they do?" He turned on his blinker.

"Commercial real estate. My husband worked with them. That's how we met."

Making a left turn, he eyed her. "So what made you decide to pull up stakes in the big city and move to Hope Crossing where there's only one stoplight?"

"Olivia. I don't want her growing up thinking everything is about money and getting ahead. I want a more modest lifestyle for her. One without privacy fences. Where she's free to run and explore and be who she wants to be instead having it dictated to her." Her comment had him wondering if she was talking more about Olivia or herself.

"Why the Christmas tree farm, though?" He made a right turn into the parking lot of the auto supply store. "I mean, you could've sold the place and moved anywhere you wanted."

"That was my initial thought, too." She shrugged. "But when I saw it for the first time, it just felt right. Like God had heard the desires of my heart, and suddenly, there it was." Pink tinged her cheeks. "I know that probably sounds strange."

"No, not at all." He parked, turned off the engine and eyed Annalise. "The Bible tells us if we delight ourselves in the Lord, He will give us the desires of our heart."

And while he wished he could believe her, experience had taught him people weren't always what they seemed. They could talk the talk without walking the walk, using others and leaving a trail of hurt in their wake. So despite everything Annalise had said, he wasn't about to let his guard down. Otherwise he'd end up falling for another sob story and coming out a chump in the end.

Chapter Five

Hawkins deposited the final trio of round bales in the hay barn Saturday morning, glad to have the task complete. Strange that bringing in hay had never bothered him before. On the contrary, he used to enjoy it. Sitting alone in the cab of the big green tractor allowed him to ponder his life. His future. But the only thing on his mind today was Annalise.

He hadn't seen or heard from her since Sunday. After exchanging the battery, their drive back to Hope Crossing had been more upbeat, with her carrying most of the conversation as she peppered him with questions about Alaska and his work there. At least she hadn't asked about his personal life.

By the time he'd finished installing the new battery and then followed her back to Bill's so she could pick up Olivia, it was nearing suppertime, so she'd been eager to get her daughter home.

Now he backed out of the barn and moved the tractor alongside the three-sided metal structure before killing the engine. At the rate things had been going, he'd expected Annalise to call with another problem. So the fact that he hadn't heard a peep all week should be good news, right?

Instead, he found himself wondering. Was she okay? Had she finished unpacking? What about the Christmas trees? She'd mentioned they were in need of maintenance. How was she going to do that with Olivia underfoot?

Don't go looking for trouble.

True that. After last week, a little distance from Annalise was a good thing. Perhaps if he kept telling himself that, he'd eventually believe it.

He hopped out of the cab and moved to the front of the barn where Justin eyed the bales that were stacked to the rafters.

"Lord willing, we'll have plenty to get us through the winter." His brother-in-law glanced at him. "They're calling for a cool front tomorrow."

Hawkins couldn't help chuckling. "Cool? You mean temps are going to dip below eighty?"

Justin narrowed his gaze. "Might tumble into the upper sixties overnight."

Pretending to shiver, Hawkins said, "I'll be sure to break out my thermals."

"All right, so it's not Alaska cold, but at least it won't be so hot."

"Okay, I'll give you that." The sun's glare had him tugging his ball cap a bit lower. "What's my sister up to today? Spending more money?" She and Justin had been slowly updating his mother's house since early summer, making it their own.

"Yes, but not until later." He glanced at his watch. "Right now she should be dropping Ky off at Annalise's. Ky's babysitting Olivia today."

"Oh?" Hawkins tried not to sound interested, even though he couldn't help wondering why Annalise might need a sitter. "I'm sure Kyleigh is thrilled. She'll get to earn a little money."

"Yeah, it's a win-win for her. She loves babies."

Hawkins' phone vibrated on his hip. Pulling it from its clip, he noted Gloriana's name on the screen. He glanced at Justin. "Any guess as to why my sister is calling me?"

Justin shook his head. "Answer it and find out."

"What's up, sissy?"

"Annalise needs your help."

Ignoring the brief thrill that shot through him, he sobered. "What's the problem?"

"The riding mower won't start, and Kyleigh is here to babysit so Annalise can do some mowing around the trees."

"I'm kind of busy."

Obviously listening, Justin twisted to face Hawkins. "Not for much longer. Gloriana and I are going shopping for a new bed in an hour."

"Come on, Hawk, it won't take that long. Besides, the mowing needs to be done before we can shear the trees. And that should've been done weeks ago."

He didn't want to come to Annalise's rescue again. And after what she'd said on their way to Brenham about not wanting him and his family to feel like she was taking advantage of them, he was fairly certain she wouldn't be too happy if he came rushing in to help either.

Maybe she had Gloriana call you so she could play the innocent.

"I have other plans." Eating lunch counted, right?

"I can't believe I'm actually having to talk you into this." His sister lowered her voice. "I'm not like Mom, trying to find ways to force you two together. You saw how overgrown things are over here. Annalise is more than happy to do it, that's why she hired Kyleigh. But if the machine won't start, she's dead in the water. It won't take you that long."

Famous last words. He didn't like being guilted, though. Especially when he knew she was right.

"Fine. I'll be there shortly."

Justin smirked as Hawkins ended the call. "What did my beautiful bride talk you into this time?"

Returning the phone to his belt, he glared at his brother-in-law. "Nothing. But my annoying sister is insisting I help Annalise get her riding mower started."

"Sounds like we finished up just in time, then." Justin elbowed him. "Not only do I have time to make myself presentable for a date with my wife, you're free to help Annalise."

Hawkins turned his back on his brother-in-law's knowing smile and headed for his truck where he turned the A/C on high and cranked the radio. And by the time he arrived at Annalise's, he was feeling rather foolish for giving Gloriana such a hard time. They'd agreed to collaborate on the tree farm, so if Annalise was willing to take on the mowing, the least he could do was make sure she had the capability.

He eyed the old wooden barn as he neared the house, noting some of the farm implements that'd been left outside and were now overrun by grass and weeds.

Then he spotted Annalise wearing a gray T-shirt over a pair of cutoffs with her hair pulled back in a ponytail that peeked out the back of a pristine pink ball cap as she sat atop the defunct mower in front of the barn, seemingly willing it to start.

Noting his sister's vehicle was nowhere to be found and wondering why he hadn't passed her along the way, he eased his truck under a nearby tree. By the time he got out, Annalise was approaching.

She moved her sunglasses to the brim of her hat, her lips pressed into a thin line. "I told Gloriana not to bother you."

"Yeah, well, we have an interest in this place, too." And as he eyed the trees in the distance, he couldn't help noticing the entire area was in need of some serious grooming. Even more so than the last time he'd seen it. Rain earlier in the week seemed to have made things worse.

"So let's see what the problem is." He followed her to the yellow mower parked just outside the barn door. "Did you make sure it had gas?"

"It started right up when I tried it the other day." She paused beside the machine, shifting from one sneaker-clad foot to the other. "After mowing the front yard with the push mower while Olivia napped, I decided to give it a try."

Lifting the hood to expose the engine, he eyed the gas tank. "You must've used up the last dregs when you did that, then, because there's nothing in there now."

Her sunglasses back in place, she crossed her arms over her chest, her cheeks suddenly pink. "They should put a gas gauge on these things."

He felt the corners of his mouth lift. "Or you could do what I did and eyeball the tank."

Her countenance fell, her focus shifting to the dirt beneath her feet as she took a step back.

Only then did he recall what she'd said about her parents and husband during their drive to Brenham. How they thought of her as incapable.

His gut tightened. Just because something was unfamiliar to her didn't mean she was incompetent. He'd hate for her to lose her confidence because of him.

"You weren't aware of that, though. Most riding mowers do have a gas gauge, just not this one." Glancing beyond the open door into the barn, he noted a blue New Holland parked just inside. That would make the task of mowing go a lot faster than the riding mower she was contemplating. "Any idea if that tractor runs?"

"Are you kidding?" She let go a nervous laugh. "I thought I was doing well testing the riding mower."

He smiled, hoping to put her at ease. Yet as he did, he found himself being prodded by the knowledge that he knew how to use one. But that would require hanging around.

And what's waiting on you back at your place? Lunch?

"Well, I noticed a shredder on my way in." He pointed to the side of the barn.

"What's that?"

"Some folks call it a rotary cutter. It's essentially a mower that attaches to the back of a tractor. And it can cover a lot more ground in a single pass than a mower." Again peering into the barn, he said, "If the tractor's working, I could man that while you use the riding mower. Get things done in a lot less time."

Her gaze drifted away from his as she toed at the ground. "I'm sure you have plenty to do at your place."

"Always. But I have an interest here, too."

She looked toward the trees, then back. "What about the gas?"

"There are bound to be some gas cans here somewhere." He moved into the barn while she followed. "If they're empty…" Eyeing three five-gallon containers against the far wall, he lifted each one and gave them a shake. "Yep. I can make a run to Plowman's and fill them up."

"Any idea what their lunch special is today?"

Gathering two containers in his right hand and the other in his left, he cast her a curious look. "No, why?"

"Because the least I can do is buy you lunch. Along with the gas, of course."

Considering the way his stomach had been grumbling... "Deal."

After letting Kyleigh know they'd be back shortly and promising to bring her lunch, too, Hawkins drove them to Plowman's where Annalise promptly swiped her card at the pump, then left him to fill the gas containers while she ran inside to grab burgers and fries, along with some cookies.

Once their stomachs and the gas tanks of their respective machines were full, Hawkins hooked the shredder to the back of the compact tractor and began mowing at one end of the property while Annalise started on the opposite side. Unlike bringing in the hay this morning, he was able to enjoy his treks up and down the rows. Not only was he confident that Annalise and Olivia were fine, he was also looking after his family's interests.

He'd done some research this week, curious as to what all was involved in Christmas-tree farming. Now as he looked at the slightly misshapen pines and cypresses, he could see that his late neighbor had been meticulous in his care of them, despite a severe case of poor judgment. What had ol' Gary been thinking when he'd moved that fence?

Despite the man's attentiveness, though, they were still looking at a lot of work. And they had better get started soon. None of them had sheared a tree before, so there'd be a learning curve. Not only that, there were *a lot* of trees. Literally thousands of them. Annalise would need all the help she could get. Not to mention the proper equipment.

Glancing at his watch, he was surprised to discover he'd been tooling around for well over an hour. Annalise's riding mower could've run out of gas by now.

He tugged his phone from his pocket and checked the screen to see if he'd missed any calls or texts. Nothing. Then again, she'd been pretty adamant about not bothering him. Perhaps he should make sure she was all right.

Reaching the end of the row, he turned toward the opposite side of the property where Annalise had been working, glancing down each and every row to see where she was. Until movement to his right had him coming to a stop.

He almost laughed out loud when he saw Annalise pulling an old red wagon that held one of the gas cans.

Turning off the tractor, he said, "Aren't you the industrious one."

She lifted a shoulder. "I ran out of gas."

"Did you forget that you own a utility vehicle?"

"If I could hoist the can into the back of it."

They were kind of heavy, even for him. He made a note to pick up a couple of gallon containers that would be more manageable for her. "You could've called me."

"I didn't want to bother you."

"I appreciate that. I really do." He almost hated to say this. "But if you couldn't get the gas can in the back of the utility vehicle, how are you going to lift it to fill the mower?"

Even with the sunglasses, he could see her countenance fall. And that tugged at his heart more than he cared to admit.

Squaring her shoulders, she looked up at him again. "Are you finished? Mowing, I mean."

"No, I came back to see how you were doing on gas. May I assist you?"

She focused on the trees, seemingly knowing she needed his help, yet not quite ready to admit it. "If we're going to get this done, I suppose I don't have a choice."

He glanced down the row, noting not only where her mower sat, but how much more of the area he'd been able to tackle with the shredder. "Sure you do."

Her gaze jerked to his.

"I can finish it by myself." He shrugged. "Your call."

Just when Annalise thought she had things under control, Hawkins had to swoop in once again and save the day. Yet while she appreciated his assistance, there was no way she was going to let him take over the job she initiated.

She'd been proud of the fact that she hadn't needed to call on anyone for help in nearly a week. And she'd been looking forward to mowing today, taking that first step toward opening the Christmas tree farm. With Kyleigh available to watch Olivia, Annalise would have plenty of time.

If only she'd thought to check the mower for gas she could have saved herself a lot of embarrassment. Instead, she'd made matters worse. Having extra gas on hand hadn't even occurred to her. The only thing she could take solace in was that refueling the riding mower the first time had lessened the weight of the container enough to where she was able to do it on her own the next two times. Even if she had spilled a little bit.

Now as she and Hawkins finished their final passes, she could only imagine what he must think of her. That she was in over her head. That she had no idea what she was doing. That she didn't have a lick of common sense, and her Christmas tree farm was doomed to fail.

Yes, the sooner she could send him on his way, the

happier she'd be. She'd endured enough embarrassment for today.

She maneuvered the riding mower back to the barn as the clock neared five, then killed the engine before making a beeline for the cooler of water she'd left in the shade near the door. After moving her sunglasses to the brim of her cap, she opened the sweaty bottle and took a drink, the cold liquid chasing away not only her thirst, but the dust that seemed to coat her mouth and throat. Not to mention her skin. She could hardly wait to grab a shower.

Recapping the bottle, she wiped the sweat from her brow with the back of her hand as Hawkins rumbled toward her on the tractor, the mower thingy trailing behind. Since it was much wider than the riding mower, he'd been able to cover twice the ground she had. Meaning if he hadn't been here, she'd still be looking at a few more hours of mowing. If she was able to finish at all. Perhaps she should learn how to operate the tractor.

After easing the machine beside the barn, he turned it off and hopped down.

She reached into the cooler, retrieving the plastic container of cookies left over from lunch, along with another water. Leaving the cookies atop the cooler, she tossed him the cold bottle as he approached in hopes quenching his thirst might supersede any desire to point out all the ways she'd failed today.

"Thanks." He twisted off the lid and took a swig while she pulled her phone from her back pocket to text Kyleigh and see how things were going.

"Help yourself to the cookies." Her thumbs continued to move over the screen as she nodded toward the small cooler.

"Don't mind if I do." He grabbed a double chocolate

chunk as the sound of gravel crunching beneath tires reached their ears.

She hit Send and peered around the barn to see Justin's truck barreling up the drive, a cloud of dust in its wake.

"How'd the shopping go?" Hawkins regarded his sister as she hopped out the passenger side a short time later.

"Great." She smiled, tucking her long, dark hair behind one ear. "We found a mattress right away."

"Leaving us plenty of time to shop for new bedroom furniture." Justin's tone seemed rather dry as he rounded the pickup.

Hawkins eyed his brother-in-law. "You don't sound very happy about that."

Slipping her arm through Justin's, Gloriana said, "He's just cranky because things took a little longer than he'd anticipated."

"A little?" Justin sent his wife an incredulous look. "I expected to be back in a couple hours."

"He's hungry, too," Gloriana whispered.

"In that case—" Annalise grabbed the cookies and passed them to Justin "—help yourself."

"Awesome. Thanks."

Gloriana stepped away from her husband and scanned the Christmas trees. "That looks so much better." Turning her attention back to Hawkins and Annalise, she scrunched her nose. "Although, it also highlights how misshapen the trees are."

"Yep." Hawkins took another drink. "And I'm afraid trimming them is going to be more time-consuming than we realize."

"Which means we need to get started on that as quick as we can," said Gloriana.

"Like when?" Hawkins grabbed the last cookie from the container Justin still held.

His sister cocked her head, her brow pinching. "How about tomorrow after church?"

"What about lunch at Mom's?"

"She can pack up everything and bring it over here," said Gloriana. "We'll tailgate. That way she and Bill can be a part of the fun, too."

"There's just one problem." Hawkins continued as they all looked at him. "None of us knows what we're doing."

This was Annalise's opportunity to prove herself. To show she knew what she was doing. Sort of, anyway.

"Actually…" Her gaze darted from the siblings to Justin and back. "I have a general idea. Gary was very detailed in his journals, and I've been studying them for months." Ever since her first visit. "He wrote everything down. What he did, when and how to do it." Turning, she motioned to the smaller red metal building not far from the barn. "And that shed right there holds all the tools we'll need."

"Then, we should check it out," said Gloriana.

"Now?" Annalise's phone vibrated in her hand, and she glanced at Kyleigh's response.

"That's not fair to Annalise." Hawkins didn't look any more pleased with the notion than she did. "She's been away from her daughter all afternoon."

"You're right." His sister looked at Annalise. "I understand if you need to get back to Olivia."

"It's not that." Kyleigh said they were doing fine. Annalise just hated the idea of leaning on the Prescotts—Hawkins, in particular—any more than needed. She'd probably worn out her welcome her first week here.

Still, if they were going to start tomorrow… "You all probably have other things to do. Besides, I've only been in that building once since arriving, and I was so overwhelmed by the amount of stuff that I decided to save it for another day."

"That's all the more reason for us to take a look," said Gloriana. "*Many hands make light work*, as my grandmother used to say."

"As if you ever listened," added Hawkins.

"That's enough out of you, Bubba." Gloriana's focus remained on Annalise. "We all have an interest here, so it only makes sense that we work together." She shrugged. "Who knows what we might find?"

Annalise glanced from a frowning Hawkins to a seemingly expectant Justin and finally Gloriana. "Follow me." Turning, she tiptoed through the ankle-high grass with Gloriana at her heels. She reached for the doorknob and gave it a twist.

Sweltering heat and stale air greeted them when they stepped inside the space that was the size of a small garage, with a roll-up door on one end. Annalise flipped the light switch as she passed, illuminating the plethora of cardboard boxes stacked throughout. A small workbench stood straight ahead, littered with more boxes.

"What *is* all this stuff?" An air of wonder laced Gloriana's question as she moved deeper into the space.

"The only things I explored are what's on the workbench. This one here—" she lifted the flaps on a long, shallow box "—contains shearing knives."

"We'll need those to shape the trees." Hawkins' statement took her by surprise. Had he done some research?

"You're correct. There are also some loppers and pruning shears." She motioned to a short stack. "These smaller boxes have things like Sold tags and ribbon."

"Ribbon?" Gloriana looked at her. "For wreaths, maybe?"

"Your guess is as good as mine." Annalise heaved a sigh. "That's as far as I got."

"I can see why." Hands on his denim-covered hips, Justin scanned the area. "This is a lot to take in."

"I see an air conditioner in the window over there." Hawkins pointed to the opposite wall. "Mind if I turn it on?"

"If you can maneuver your way through the maze of boxes, be my guest," said Annalise.

"We need to inventory what all is here." While her brother picked his way across the room, Gloriana gathered her long hair into a ponytail, then secured it with an elastic band she pulled off her wrist. "I can do that on my phone if you all want to start unpacking and tell me what you find."

As the A/C kicked on, Justin eyed his wife. "You can add *shaker* to the list." He pointed to a large box with its contents printed on the side.

"Whatever that is," Gloriana said as she typed.

"It's used to shake a tree after it's been cut to rid it of any loose needles and such."

"Critters, too." Hawkins reached for another box, chuckling.

"Let's hope not." Annalise pulled out packing material and stared inside the next container. "I have no idea what this is."

Gloriana peered over her shoulder. "Is there a packing list?"

"Yep." Annalise pulled it out. "Says it's a garland-making machine."

"They make a machine for that?" Gloriana held up a hand for a high five. "I have a feeling that's going to save us a lot of time."

"Tree stands over here." Hawkins stood near the air

conditioner. "*Lots* of them. Which doesn't make sense. Aren't the people supposed to cut their own trees?"

"Yes." Annalise wiped the sweat from her brow before opening the next box. "But they'll need a stand to put it in once they get it home. If they don't already have one."

"Marketing 101. If we have them here," said Gloriana, "they won't need to go someplace else to purchase one. Which reminds me." She looked at Annalise. "Have you applied for a sales tax license?"

"Earlier this week. According to the website, I should have it in a few weeks."

"Perfect." Gloriana smiled. "Does that mean you have a name for the tree farm? I could use it for branding."

"Gary and Eileen were planning to call it Hope Crossing Christmas Tree Farm, so I went with that."

"I think that's a great idea. Lets people know where it is, and it helps promote the town. And that benefits everyone."

With all four of them working to determine what was in the shed, the task was completed in a little over an hour. Much less time than Annalise had feared.

Gloriana eyed the list she'd compiled on her phone. "Gary was obviously serious about opening his tree farm to the public. From what I can tell, he's got everything we could possibly need. Or close to it, anyway."

"Too bad he resorted to stealing to do it." Hawkins moved alongside her to look at the list.

While Annalise cringed from the sting of his comment, his sister promptly elbowed him. "Might I remind you, big brother, that all things work together for good to those who love the Lord."

"Okay, so we have all this stuff." He removed his cap and scratched a hand through his dark hair. "We still don't know what we're doing when it comes to shaping those trees."

"Yes, we do," said Annalise. "And the process is called shearing."

They all looked at her.

"Not that I've actually implemented any of that knowledge yet." She sucked in a bolstering breath. "I wasn't exaggerating when I said Gary's journals were detailed." She shrugged. "We could go over his notes, so we'll all have a better idea of what to expect."

"That's not a bad idea," said Gloriana.

"Now?" Justin rubbed his belly. "I'm starving."

Gloriana checked her watch. "I really hate to lose this momentum we've got going, but I guess it is suppertime."

"Not to mention the Aggies will be taking the field shortly."

Gloriana waved off her brother. "Annalise, what would you think about me grabbing some pizzas so we could eat here and go over the journals together?"

"Hope Crossing has a pizza place?"

"No, I'll have to run to Brenham."

"That'll take forever." Justin didn't seem too crazy about the idea. He was hungry now, and it would take almost an hour to go to Brenham and back.

While Annalise agreed that it would be best for all of them to have some sort of idea about shearing prior to tomorrow, she didn't want to take up any more of their time than necessary.

"How does lasagna and garlic bread sound?" She'd made a big pan last night and was planning to portion out the rest and freeze it. "I have plenty for everyone."

"That sounds amazing," said Gloriana.

"You had me at *lasagna*." Justin smiled.

Gloriana shifted her attention to Hawkins. "What do you say, Hawk? Are you in?"

When he hesitated, Annalise said, "I'd be happy to give you sole possession of the TV remote so you can watch your game."

His smile was a slow one. "In that case, what are we waiting for?"

Chapter Six

Annalise awoke Sunday morning feeling as though her arm muscles had been shredded. She thought toting Olivia around all these months would have strengthened her but steering that mower yesterday had proven her wrong. A dose of ibuprofen before heading out the door to church had helped, however, and as she gathered now with the entire Prescott family for a tailgate lunch of pulled pork sandwiches, deviled eggs and coleslaw at the edge of the freshly mown field of Christmas trees, she could hardly wait to get to work.

"The pork is delicious, Francie." Beneath the portable canopy Justin and Hawkins had set up near the trio of trucks, Annalise eyed the woman holding Olivia in the camp chair beside hers. "It appears my daughter approves, too."

"She has good taste." Francie gave the child a squeeze. "Don't you, sweetie?" After dropping a kiss atop Olivia's head, she fed her another bite. "This meat is so easy to fix. You simply season it, put it in a covered pot, then cook it low and slow so the flavors have a chance to become one with the pork." Using a napkin, she wiped sauce from her finger. "This one cooked all night."

"That does sound easy. I don't suppose you'd share your recipe."

"Of course, dear."

"I'm ready for a slice of your chocolate sheet cake." Hawkins eyed his mother from the back of Bill's truck.

"Help yourself. It's in the cooler, and I've already cut it into squares." Her dark gaze remained on her son. "Careful, though. You eat too much, and you'll be ready for a nap instead of shearing."

Last evening, Annalise, Hawkins, Justin and Gloriana had pored over Uncle Gary's journals, trying to understand the shearing process. After watching a few videos online, everyone felt as though they had a better idea of what to do, but they had yet to actually attempt it. Now the time had come to take what little knowledge they had and put it into action, bringing her dream another step closer.

Yet as she envisioned people wandering through the trees, looking for that perfect specimen, her dream was marred by the reality of the shaggy examples that stood before her. What if they couldn't make them look just so?

Standing, she tucked her plate and napkin into the trash bag Francie had brought, then stared out over the trees while clouds thickened overhead, offering a reprieve from the midday heat. "I think we should start in the back with some of the smaller trees until we get the hang of things." Turning, she addressed the group. "I'd hate to butcher one of these large trees up front when they'll be the first thing people see."

"Excellent idea." Gloriana approached, plate in hand. "And by starting with the smaller ones, they'll have plenty of time to recover from any flaws we might inflict."

"My thoughts exactly," said Annalise.

With shearing knives in the back of her utility vehicle, Annalise, Gloriana and Kyleigh made their way toward the back of the property while Justin, Hawkins and Bill followed in the vehicle Justin had trailered over from Prescott Farms. Since Olivia was rubbing her eyes, a sure sign she was tired, Francie had offered to stay with her at the house.

"Annalise, you should go first." Gloriana passed her a shearing knife a short time later, sending a wave of panic through Annalise.

"Why me?"

"Because this is your place. Your dream." Gloriana smiled beneath the brim of her ball cap. "And you've done more research than the rest of us."

Drawing in a deep breath, Annalise gripped the handle of the lengthy razor-edged blade. "Okay, but I'd better not hear any laughing."

She approached a five-foot tree that looked as though it was having a bad-hair day with random limbs sticking out all over. "They said to top the tree first to create the point." She pulled clippers from her back pocket and snipped off a couple of stray shoots. Then, taking a step back, she surveyed the entire tree, her gaze moving up and down as she tried to envision the perfect shape.

"Here goes nothing, so y'all stand back." Lifting the blade, she swung it like a sword, working from top to bottom, then paused to evaluate her work. Satisfied, she continued until she'd gone around the entire tree.

"That looks great." Gloriana clapped her hands. "Are you sure you haven't done this before, Annalise?"

"Never." She rubbed her shoulder. If she thought her muscles were sore this morning, she'd probably be dying tomorrow. "That's one down, thousands more to go."

Why had she said that? The mere thought sent a wave of panic racing through her. "Who's next?"

Gloriana eyed her brother. "Go for it, Hawk."

He moved alongside a similar-sized tree and repeated what Annalise had done without saying a word. Actually, he hadn't said much to her all day, though he'd seemed to enjoy himself as he played with Olivia earlier. But then, Olivia was still a baby. She was cute and did funny things, while her mother's forte seemed to be finding herself indebted to others.

Hawkins had come over yesterday after his sister all but demanded he help Annalise start the riding mower and then ended up staying until after dark. Something she was fairly certain he was still kind of miffed about. Even if he had offered to help her with the mowing. Like he'd said, though, he had a vested interest.

"Not bad." Gloriana admired his work.

After everyone had made an initial attempt without issue, they spread out, each practicing on a few more small trees.

Satisfied they were getting the hang of things, Annalise said, "We may as well move on to the trees we plan to harvest this year. There are a lot of them, far more than we can do in a single day, but we'll knock out what we can." Hopefully it would be a noticeable amount.

As they set to work, Annalise somehow managed to stay focused on what she was doing instead of watching the others. And after creating several handsome trees all by herself, she seemed to fall into a nice little groove. It felt good to finally make some progress. Yet as the clouds morphed from a pale gray to pewter a couple hours later, her stomach began to churn. No, it couldn't rain. Not now. If they didn't make some significant headway today with all of them working, they might not have enough inventory to open this year, and she was counting on that money to pay the taxes on the farm.

Thunder rumbled in the distance as she finished yet another seven-footer. She straightened, her eyes burning. She'd been at this for over two hours and had only completed, maybe, fifty trees. If everyone else moved at the same pace, that would only be two hundred and fifty trees. That was barely a dent in the thousands that spread across the property.

Her phone buzzed in her back pocket. She pulled it out, her vision blurring as she read the text from Hawkins.

Storm's rolling in. Time to get inside.

It pained her to admit he was right. If it was just her, she'd keep working, but she couldn't put other people at risk.

She hurried toward the end of the row where she'd parked the utility vehicle, hollering for Gloriana and Kyleigh to follow as she passed. The mother–daughter team had been working together on an adjacent row. No sooner had they ducked under the vehicle's roof than the rain let loose.

Minutes later, Annalise pulled up to the front porch. "You two go on in while I put this is the garage."

They rushed up the steps as she made a U-turn and aimed for the garage.

Hawkins had obviously beaten her back, because his vehicle was already there, beads of water dripping onto the concrete floor.

She parked beside it and got out as rain pummeled the metal roof, drowning out every other sound. Pausing, she stared out the window that faced the Christmas trees. A gust of cool air swept into the space from the open roll-up doors opposite, and she wrapped her arms around herself. Why had she thought she could do this?

For once in your life, use a little common sense, Annalise, her mother's voice echoed in her mind. *This is foolishness. What do you know about running a business, let alone a Christmas tree farm?*

Coming here had been a mistake. After all, reading about something wasn't the same as doing it. She'd obviously underestimated the amount of work involved.

Tears pricked her eyes before spilling onto her cheeks.

"There you are." Hawkins' raised voice startled her.

She quickly swiped at her tears as he stepped in front of her.

"I wondered where you—" His gaze bore into her, his expression softening. "What's wrong?"

"I can't do this."

He cupped her elbows in his palms, his warmth seeping into her. Confusion marred his handsome face. "Do what?"

"I'm not capable of running a Christmas tree farm."

"What?" He took a step back. "Why would you think that?"

"Oh, come on." She shivered. "I didn't even look to see if there was gas in the mower."

Hands now on his hips, he shook his head. "Have you forgotten about our collaboration? Our agreement?"

"It doesn't matter." They hadn't signed a formal agreement yet, anyway. "Even my two-thirds of the trees are still too much."

He dipped his head, urging her to look at him. "You do realize we're playing catch-up right now? But we will catch up. Once we do that, the maintenance won't be nearly as overwhelming."

"There were six of us working today, and we barely

made a dent." To her chagrin, tears fell again, and she turned away.

After a moment, he moved in front of her. "Between Gary's journals and preparation and your ideas to make this a real destination for families, I have no doubt that you *can* do this, Annalise. You've got my entire family excited about this endeavor. Including me."

His words washed over her like a healing balm, soothing her disbelieving heart. No one had ever spoken such encouraging words to her before. Though she couldn't help wondering if Hawkins truly believed what he was saying or if he was simply placating her. Saying what he thought she wanted to hear.

He momentarily removed his ball cap, just long enough to rake his fingers through his thick hair. "Look, I've got another week before I have to go back to work. Even then, I'll be working from Prescott Farms. I can help you. We'll focus on the sections that are ready to be harvested this year."

"But what about Olivia? She's not scheduled to start day care for two more weeks when I go back to work." Though she didn't necessarily have a set schedule. Doing her computer work in the evening wasn't uncommon.

"We could check with my mother. I have a feeling she'd be thrilled to babysit. Gloriana might be willing to pitch in, too." He smiled then. "Everyone's smitten with Olivia." Himself included, from what Annalise had witnessed. The way he interacted with her daughter never failed to make her smile.

"I don't know. I'd hate for them to feel like—"

"Like you're taking advantage of them, I know. And I assure you, they won't." He took her chilled fingers into his warm hands. "Look, we were only at this for a couple of hours today. Yeah, it's going to take a lot more time, and yes, it's going to be hard work, but I believe in you, Annalise. Just think of all the smiling faces that'll be roaming this place weeks from now as they search for that perfect tree." His confidence in her was as bolstering as it was attractive.

The rain eased slightly as she cast another glance toward the trees. Almost two weeks ago she'd packed up her life and her daughter and moved to Hope Crossing, confident this was her home, her dream and her daughter's legacy. Was she ready to throw all of that away and give up just because things were proving to be tougher than she'd imagined? Or did she want to be a role model for her daughter, instilling in Olivia that with determination and hard work she could do anything she set her mind to?

She didn't need to give it a second thought. "I hope you enjoy Christmas music, because you're going to be hearing a lot of it in the coming weeks."

Hawkins never could stand to see a girl cry. As a boy, it used to tear him apart to listen to Gloriana's tearful pleas when their father wouldn't allow her to accompany them whenever they'd head out to work cattle, hunt or fish. So much so that when they got back, Hawkins would try to make it up to his sister by inviting her to do something with him.

Now that he was a man, a woman's tears still seemed to be his kryptonite. First Bridget, now Annalise.

He supposed that wasn't a fair comparison, though. Aside from that first day at Plowman's, Annalise hadn't asked him for a thing. And the one time she had, it was only because she'd had no other choice.

But since then, she hadn't made one request of him.

Even when his mother or sister had volunteered him to assist her, she'd seemed unhappy about it.

Now as he stood amid rows of Virginia pines just before eight thirty Monday morning, waiting for her to return from his mother's after dropping off Olivia, he knew he'd done the right thing in offering to help. Annalise wasn't the only one looking forward to opening the tree farm to the public. Gloriana had been hard at work on a promotional campaign. She'd done wonders for Hope Crossing's annual fair and rodeo this past spring, bringing in folks from all across the state. And while the scope for the tree farm was significantly smaller, she seemed confident that she could garner plenty of exposure that would create a lot of interest.

Armed with a shearing knife, he attacked his fourth tree of the morning. Moving it this way and that, he felt a bit like a swashbuckler. When he took a step back to evaluate his latest conquest, notes of Bing Crosby's "White Christmas" carried on the gentle morning breeze.

Turning, he saw Annalise coming toward him wearing a pair of skinny jeans and a *Merry Christmas* T-shirt, a shearing knife in one hand and an all-too enticing smile on her face.

"I didn't hear you drive up."

"That's because I'm stealthy, like a ninja." Stepping back, she struck a silly pose, wielding her makeshift sword.

He couldn't contain his laughter. He hadn't seen this playful side of her before. And after all the struggles she'd faced since arriving in Hope Crossing, it did his heart good.

"I don't think ninjas play Christmas music on their phone."

Straightening, she stepped in front of him, close enough

that he caught the aroma of what he was coming to think of as her trademark floral fragrance. "They do if they're North Pole ninjas." The mischief that sparkled in her blue eyes had him taking a step back.

This fun, playful Annalise was way too captivating. He eyed the cloudless sky. Justin had been right about the front. It had moved in behind yesterday's storm, leaving them with cooler, dryer air.

Feeling composed once again, he dared a glance her way. "All right, my little ninja warrior, let's get to work."

"Aye aye, Captain." Smiling, she sent him a mock salute before moving to the trees on the opposite side of the row he'd been working.

Meanwhile, he just stood there, dumbfounded, wondering what had gotten into her. He'd never seen her this animated before. So carefree. His little pep talk yesterday hadn't been that good, had it?

They completed their first row with little to no conversation. Annalise sang along with the holiday music that continued to spill from her back pocket, while he occasionally hummed, though not loud enough for her to hear. Though, it got him to thinking that they should have some music playing around the tree farm when it was open to the public. Something to add to the festive mood.

As they neared the end of the second row, a pickup truck pulled alongside the garage.

Hawkins stopped what he was doing. "Are you expecting someone?"

She looked from the vehicle to him, her expression wary. "No."

Moments later, a gentleman emerged, stocky build with streaks of gray peppering his brown hair. And he seemed to have a keen interest in the Christmas trees.

Hawkins stepped in front of Annalise. "You stay here

while I find out what he wants." She complied, but he could feel her gaze at his back every step of the way.

Obviously sensing his approach, the man turned, and as Hawkins drew closer, he thought he recognized the man.

"Hawkins Prescott! Don't tell me you bought ol' Gary's place."

His eyes widened. "Mr. Ballard?"

The man chuckled. "Son, you're likely nearing forty by now. Go ahead and call me Tom." His former teacher met Hawkins halfway and they shook hands.

"What are you doing here?" Hawkins had heard the man had moved away from Hope Crossing after retiring.

"I was just out for a drive. I live in Brenham now, but I used to come out here and help Gary with his trees on occasion." The man shrugged. "Thought I'd pop by and see if anyone was livin' here yet." Tom cast a glance toward Annalise. "That the missus?"

"Oh, no." Hawkins shook his head. "I'm not married."

"That's a shame. She's a pretty one."

Nothing like stating the obvious. "That's Annalise. Gary left the place to her and her daughter. Well, to his nephew anyway, but he's also deceased. Hold on." He turned toward Annalise, motioning for her to join them.

"I'd like you to meet Tom Ballard," he said as she reached his side. "He was my tenth-grade algebra teacher."

"It's nice to meet you." She smiled.

"Pleased to make your acquaintance." The older man nodded.

Addressing Annalise, Hawkins said, "Tom says he used to help Gary with the trees."

"Really?" Interest sparked in her eyes.

"Yes, ma'am. My granddaddy grew Christmas trees back when I was growing up in North Carolina, so I'd had a fair amount of experience." He pointed to the shear-ing knife in Annalise's hand. "Looks like you're doing some shearing."

"Yes, sir. I just moved in a couple of weeks ago, and things are a little overgrown."

"I'm sure they are. Haven't been tended since early spring. The good news is that Gary kept on top of things right up to his passing." He eyed Annalise. "I reckon the gas-powered trimmer is a little heavy for you to manage."

She shifted from one foot to the next. "I've seen them in some of the videos I've watched online but haven't thought about purchasing one yet."

Tom looked at her strangely. "What do you mean? There's one in the barn. Gary and I used it almost ex-clusively."

Hawkins was pretty sure his expression matched Annalise's wide-eyed, mouth-agape one.

"I'd be happy to show you," said Tom.

They moved briskly to the barn where he went straight to the spot where it hung on the wall.

After adding some fresh gas, they returned to the trees where Tom zipped through several in the blink of an eye.

"That's amazing." Annalise slid her hands into the pockets of her jeans. "It's obvious you know what you're doing."

Her phone rang then, and she excused herself to an-swer it.

"Why don't you give it a try?" Tom handed Hawkins the machine. "Use a light touch until you get a feel for it."

Hawkins raised the machine that wasn't much more than a hedge trimmer on a pole. Starting at the top, he did his best to mimic Tom's moves until he'd completed the tree. Though not nearly as quickly as Tom had done.

"Not bad," said the older man.

Annalise approached, her smile gone. "That was your mom." She looked at Hawkins, her brow puckering. "Olivia is sick."

"What's wrong? Does she need to go to a doctor?"

"She threw up and is running a fever. It's probably just a bug. I'll monitor her for a while."

He thought of the precious baby who was always ready with a smile. "Poor kid."

"I hate to leave, but I need to go get her."

"Of course." He passed the trimmer back to Tom. "Would you like me to go with you?"

"That's not necessary. One of us needs to keep working. Besides, I'd hate to expose you to anything."

"You drive safe, then. And don't rush. Mom knows how to care for a sick baby."

As she turned away, he faced his former teacher. "Olivia is her one-year-old daughter."

"No wonder she's worried."

As Annalise sped away, Tom addressed Hawkins. "So what are her plans for the tree farm?"

"She wants to have it open for business the day after Thanksgiving. And it's not just her. My family, too." Though Hawkins didn't feel the need to explain why. Tom and Gary were friends. No point in tarnishing Gary's memory by mentioning the land.

"Too bad ol' Gary couldn't be here to see it. Sounds like he left things in the right hands, though." He looked around. "However, if you expect to have all of these trees ready to go, you've got your work cut out for you."

Hands on his hips, Hawkins let go a sigh. "You're telling me. That's why we're out here today." And tomorrow, and the next day, until they at least had a decent inventory.

"Well…" Tom seemed to search the field before him

"…I find myself mighty bored lately. There's only so much a fella can do with a small yard in the city. Being out here invigorates me, though. Always has. Must be those childhood memories it brings back." He eyed Hawkins. "I'd be happy to offer my services."

"Are you serious?"

"As a heart attack." The man chuckled at his own joke.

"Tom, that would be great." And worth any amount of money, at this point. "That would free Annalise up to start prepping the rest of the place."

"You, too."

Hawkins looked at the man. "You really think I'd leave you to do the shearing all by yourself?"

Tom shrugged. "Wouldn't be the first time. I kept things up when Gary's wife was sick." He tilted his head to face Hawkins. "I work quickly, and I enjoy it." His faded green eyes surveyed the property. "I always thought Gary's idea to open a Christmas tree farm was a good one, so I'm looking forward to seeing it actually happen."

They briefly discussed compensation.

After shaking hands, Tom said, "Y'all are in a time crunch not only to get things open but to tend to all the preparations that go along with it. Once this season is over, though, things won't seem so overwhelming. You'll be able to stay on top of the maintenance, so this time next year things won't be nearly as stressful."

"That would be a good thing for all of us." Hawkins' enthusiasm had grown exponentially as they went back to work. He could hardly wait to tell Annalise she no longer had to worry about the trees. And anything he could do to relieve her stress was a good thing, indeed.

Chapter Seven

"I'm sorry you're sick, sweet pea." Annalise smoothed a hand over her lethargic daughter's still-warm forehead before unbuckling her from her car seat.

Olivia didn't protest and promptly snuggled against Annalise's chest as they emerged from her vehicle into an otherwise beautiful, sunny day.

"Sweet baby girl." Resting her cheek against the child's head, she bumped the back door with her hip to close it before starting toward the house. "Let's get you some medicine so you can feel better."

Annalise had been kicking herself all the way to and from Francie's for not thinking to put some children's acetaminophen in the diaper bag. Not to mention wondering if she'd been so focused on getting to the trees this morning that she hadn't recognized Olivia was feeling bad. Surely she would have noticed if she'd felt warm, though.

She continued toward the kitchen door, noting that Tom's red pickup was still there. Perhaps he was giving Hawkins some more tips on how to use the trimmer. She still couldn't believe they'd had one all along and never realized it.

Inside, she hurried to the cupboard beside the sink with Olivia on her hip. Opening the cabinet door, she grabbed the medicine and a syringe as Olivia began to whimper against her shoulder.

"I know, baby. Mama's hurrying." After awkwardly measuring a dose, she continued down the short hall-way to Olivia's bedroom and laid her atop the changing table before retrieving the infant thermometer from the drawer below.

Annalise momentarily set the device inside her daughter's ear then checked the reading, her anxiety increasing when she saw 101.6 degrees.

Why hadn't she noticed anything earlier this morning? But then, this wasn't the first time Olivia had gone from zero to fifty in terms of an illness. No warning, just suddenly sick. And it was likely the fever that had caused her to throw up.

Poor Francie. That certainly wasn't what she'd signed on for when she agreed to watch Olivia.

Annalise gave the child her medicine and had set to work changing her diaper when she heard a knock on the kitchen door.

Suspecting it was Hawkins, she turned toward the hall. "Come on in."

Olivia startled at her raised voice, her blue eyes filling with tears.

"It's okay, sweetie. Mama was just talking to Mr. Hawkins." She used her baby voice, hoping to fend off the cry that was about to follow, then promptly affixed the diaper tabs and scooped the child into her arms as the sound of boots on the hardwood reached her ears.

"Who's that, Olivia?" She turned so her daughter could see him at the opposite end of the hall. And while the child failed to display her usual enthusiasm, any melt-down seemed to have been averted.

"How is she?" His gaze remained fixed on Olivia as they approached, stopping beside him.

"Not too good. She's definitely got a fever, which means I'm going to need to get her to the doctor."

Looking at Annalise, he smoothed a hand across Olivia's back. "Do you have one yet?"

"Not here."

"Unfortunately, the closest *here* is Brenham."

"I had a feeling." She should have taken time out that first week to find and settle on a doctor instead of waiting until she needed one. Granted that first week had been a rather chaotic time, but it wasn't like anyone ever planned for a child to get sick.

"I don't suppose you know anyone who could recommend a pediatrician, do—?" She caught herself. "Oh, wait. Tori. We exchanged numbers last week." She awkwardly tugged her phone from her back pocket. "I'll ask her who she uses for Aiden."

"Would you like me to take Olivia?"

Looking up, she saw a compassion in Hawkins' gaze that took her by surprise.

"That is, if she'll let me hold her," he continued. "I know how little ones tend to prefer their mamas when they're sick."

"Let's find out." She looked at her daughter. "You want to go see Mr. Hawkins for little bit?" To her surprise, her daughter lifted her head.

He tentatively reached for her. "What do you think? Shall we let your mom make a phone call?"

Annalise wasn't sure who was more surprised when Olivia leaned into his waiting arms.

"Wow, you really are feverish." His cheek resting on her daughter's head, he moved into the living room.

"I gave her some medicine right before you came in, so it hasn't had time to work yet."

As he settled into the rocking chair with Olivia, Annalise dialed Tori only to have it go to voice mail. Then she remembered Tori was a schoolteacher. So she sent a text instead, in hopes Tori might be able to respond.

In the meantime, she opened her laptop on the kitchen counter to search for nearby pediatricians. She'd just begun typing her first query into the search engine when Tori responded.

Sorry about Olivia. Poor baby. Dr. Minard in Brenham is great. I'm sure she'll squeeze you in.

Annalise sure hoped so.

She was about to search for the doctor's info when Tori sent the link to her website and phone number.

"Yes!"

"Did you meet with success?" Hawkins' quiet voice wafted from the living room.

"With Tori, yes. Now I just need to call the doctor." She tapped on the number Tori had sent and pressed the phone to her ear. A few minutes later, Olivia was on the books for three o'clock, thanks to a well-timed cancellation.

Finally able to catch her breath, Annalise moved into the living room to find her daughter asleep in Hawkins' arms while he continued to move the chair to and fro. Olivia's chubby cheeks were flushed, and Annalise sent up a silent prayer for her fever to break soon.

"We have an appointment at three," she told Hawkins.

"Glad to hear it." Why did he have to look so natural

holding Olivia? As if he'd been doing it since the moment she entered this world. Something Dylan had never mastered, and he was her father. He'd always been awkward with Olivia. Disinterested, if Annalise was honest.

Not happy with the train of thought her mind had jumped on, she said, "I saw Tom's truck was still here when I arrived. Did he leave?"

"No, he's out there working on the trees."

"I hope you're not taking advantage of him." She gathered this morning's coffee cup from the side table and started for the kitchen.

"Not at all. I hired him."

Her heart stuttered to a stop along with her feet. She turned, her insides twisting as her ire sparked. "I-I'm sorry. You what?"

He adjusted her daughter slightly. "He offered to assist us, so I hired him."

Willing a calm she didn't necessarily feel at the moment, she stared at him. "Don't you think you should have checked with me first?"

"It's okay. I can pay him, and then we'll just take the expense off the top before we divvy things up at the end of the season."

Something churned in her gut. A burning sensation. "But I don't even know the man. Now you've given him carte blanche to my property. Do I need to remind you that I'm a single mother?"

"Calm down. Tom is a good guy. And with him taking care of the trees, you'll have more time to focus on getting everything else ready." He glanced down at her daughter, smoothing a hand over her downy hair. "Trust me. This is a good thing."

Annalise felt her eyes widen. Her body stiffened. How many times had Dylan said the same thing? And in each and every instance she'd blindly followed his lead. Then he'd died, leaving her to deal with the fallout of his bad decisions.

You saw how fast Tom sheared those trees.

But what if he's not as good a person as Hawkins claimed?

He was a teacher. And like Hawkins said, you could use the extra time to start clearing and staging things for the opening.

Hastily retreating to the kitchen before she said something she'd regret, she set the cup on the counter with a little more force than necessary and willed herself to take a deep breath. As she exhaled, she thought about yesterday and the meltdown she'd had over all there was to do. The fear that she wouldn't be able to do it all. Until Hawkins had convinced her otherwise. She'd gone to bed last night praying he was right.

Her shoulders slumped as her anger melted in regret. What if Tom was the answer to her prayers? Still, Hawkins could have checked with her first.

What would you have said?

The realization that she probably would have concurred with him had her feeling rather small.

She returned to the opening between the kitchen and living room. "Hawkins, I—"

"You're right." He looked up at her with those dark eyes that never failed to draw her in. "I should've run the idea past you before giving him an answer. I'm sorry. If you want me to tell him I've changed my mind, I will."

That was about as unexpected as the warm fuzzy feelings fluttering about her insides like a swarm of butterflies.

"No, that won't be necessary."

She swallowed the lump in her throat, reminding herself that Hawkins was nothing like Dylan. And realizing just how dangerous that revelation could be to her heart.

By Wednesday morning, no one would've guessed Olivia had even had an ear infection. Standing outside of the rustic barn he and Annalise hoped to clear out today, Hawkins watched the happy child toddle toward him alongside her mother just after eight, a smile on her face as she clapped her chubby little hands and jabbered something undecipherable.

The scene did his heart good. Holding her listless, fever-ravaged body a couple of days ago had torn at his heart and had him wondering if that was what it was like to be a father. The role was one he'd always hoped to have, yet here he was, pushing forty, and God had yet to bring the right woman into his life. Someone who'd appreciate his tender heart instead of abusing it. A woman who enjoyed the simple things in life and didn't pretend to be something she wasn't. A woman who'd love him for who he was and not what he could do for her.

His gaze inadvertently shifted to Annalise. Despite her objections, hiring Tom had been the right decision. Not that her concerns weren't valid, and, looking back, Hawkins regretted not discussing things with her before giving Tom the go-ahead. Still, with Tom focused on the trees, there was one less thing for Annalise to worry about.

More and more, Hawkins found himself wanting to alleviate her burdens and see more of the bubbly, light-hearted woman who'd worked alongside him before the news about her daughter had again weighed her down.

On second thought, that particular side of Annalise could easily sneak past his defenses, so he'd best be careful what he wished for.

Under a cloudless sky, he lowered the brim of his ball cap and shook off his wandering thoughts as Olivia continued toward him with a toothy grin.

"Somebody is in a good mood this morning." He lowered himself to one knee. A move that had the child picking up speed, her smile even bigger as she headed straight for him. He never would have imagined one little person could spark so much joy.

Lifting her into his arms, he pushed to his feet to greet her mother. The dark circles so evident yesterday had all but disappeared and been replaced with a killer smile that had her blue eyes sparkling.

"Make that two somebodies." Annalise stopped beside him, clad in a pair of well-worn skinny jeans, a faded-blue T-shirt and a pair of once-white sneakers that had seen better days. She held a small plastic container in one hand. "We both went to bed early and slept straight through the night."

Thankful for the distraction of her daughter, he tickled Olivia, eliciting the cutest belly laugh. "Did you get some good rest?"

"We even had time to make pumpkin spice muffins this morning." Annalise held out the container. "I brought you a few."

"Awesome. I love pumpkin spice." He stood Olivia beside him before taking hold of the container and opening it. The scents of cinnamon, ginger and a hint of cloves awakened his appetite, despite the two microwaved sausage biscuits he'd downed before heading over here.

He removed one and took a bite as they heard a vehicle coming up the drive. A moment later, his mother's white Tahoe came into view. She waved before continuing beneath the live oak near the house.

Olivia seemed to watch intently. And when his mother emerged from the vehicle, the child smiled. "'Cee?"

Annalise smoothed a hand over her daughter's hair. "Yep, that's Mrs. Francie."

By the time his mother joined them, he wasn't sure whose smile was bigger, Mom's or Olivia's.

Still licking crumbs from his fingers, he eyed his mother. "What brings you by?"

Now holding the child, she said, "This little gingersnap." She kissed Olivia's cheek. "I called Annalise earlier and offered to come over and watch her so you two could get some work done without little miss here underfoot."

Given that he'd be heading back to work in a few days, he appreciated his mother's willingness to help.

She eyed him as he pulled out a second muffin. "Whatcha got there?" She inhaled. "Smells like pumpkin spice."

The only one in their family who loved pumpkin spice more than him was his mother. "Yes, and they're mine, so back off."

"But there are plenty more in the house," Annalise was quick to inject. "So you can help yourself to as many as you'd like, Francie."

"Wait," he said, "how come I only get three, then?"

Annalise shrugged. "That's all that would fit in the container."

Still holding Olivia, his mother said, "Y'all ready to tackle the barn?"

"Yes, ma'am." Annalise gathered her hair into a short ponytail and looped it through an elastic band. "And I suppose we'd best get to it."

"All right, then." Mom turned, carrying Olivia. "We'll be in the house if you need us." Glancing over her shoulder, she smirked at Hawkins. "Eating as many pumpkin spice muffins as we can get our hands on."

"Mom…"

Annalise placed a hand on his arm, sending a jolt of awareness straight to his core. "Easy now. She's just kidding."

His eyes locked with hers. A move he instantly regretted. Looking into their blue depths had him longing to linger. To get to know Annalise better. To see her smile and hear her laugh.

But there was work to be done.

He cleared his throat and stepped away. "Just as well. Too many muffins'll make me lazy, and we've got work to do." He moved to the wood doors he'd opened wide when he first arrived, taking in the cluttered expanse from timeworn rafters to dirt floor. The front of the space was to serve as the welcome center when people arrived at the tree farm, so their goal was to bring at least some semblance of order to the space.

"Where do we even begin?" She stood beside him. He didn't have to look to know she was there. Her floral fragrance gave her away. And he didn't dare look at her again.

"Let's start by removing the big stuff." He moved inside. "I'll get the tractor, you take the riding mower."

Once those were outside, the push mower and gas cans were next.

"What about these?" Annalise pointed to the collection of garden tools hanging on the wall. Rakes, shovels, a hoe, a posthole digger, a Weed eater and more.

"Since they're not in our way, we'll leave them for now."

Dust motes danced in the sunlight that peered through gaps in the weathered wood walls as they traipsed in and out over the next few hours, lugging countless paint cans, galvanized tubs and buckets along with half-empty bags of potting soil and fertilizer. A crude L-shaped workbench in a far corner was littered with wrenches, screwdrivers and a multitude of other hand tools, not to mention a couple of rusted metal coffee cans containing random nails and screws.

"What about that stuff?"

He turned from the workbench to see Annalise pointing overhead to an array of items sitting atop a sheet of particleboard that spanned the rafters. The only item he could really see from his vantage point, though, was a large plastic snowman wearing a black top hat, a red-and-green scarf and a wide grin. "That snowman looks like he might fall into the vintage category."

"I was thinking the same thing." She looked at him now. "Depending what condition he's in, we might be able to use him in our decorating."

"Let's go ahead and bring it all down." Hawkins scanned the space until he spotted an eight-foot wooden ladder leaning against a side wall. He retrieved it before settling it near Annalise.

"Are you sure that's sturdy enough?"

With the side supports in place, he tested it. "It should be fine."

"Famous last words."

Smiling at her comment, he continued up the rungs until he was eye level with the items. He swiped away the cobwebs. "It appears that Frosty isn't the only Christmas decoration up here."

"Oh, yeah?"

"Looks like some wooden cutouts, too." He tilted his head for a better view. "Reindeer, maybe."

"I'd like to have a closer look at that snowman if you can get him down here."

"Hold the ladder," he said as he moved up another rung. He stretched, leaning against the crossbeam as he took hold of four-foot Frosty and tugged him closer.

He looked down at Annalise. "I don't think I can carry him down. He's too bulky. And while I'm tempted to just let him fall, I'm afraid he might shatter."

"We don't want that."

"No." He surveyed the space below. "Hand me one of those ropes over there." He pointed toward a corner. "The longest one you can find."

Moments later, she took two steps up the ladder and handed one to him. "What are you going to do?"

"Make a lasso so I can lower him down to you." He cinched a loop and knot at one end, then threaded the other end through the loop before sliding the whole thing over Frosty's torso. Once it was around his ample midsection, Hawkins tightened the rope just enough that it wouldn't slip off. At least, that was the plan.

"All right." He eased the decoration over the edge. "Are you ready?"

"Yep." She reached her hands in the air as he slowly began to lower their captive. "Almost there," she said a few moments later. "Got him!"

Hawkins let go of the rope.

Annalise stumbled backward. "Whoa…" Just when he thought she'd recovered and started down the ladder, he heard her say, "Uh-oh."

He glanced down as she fell backward. "Annalise!" Two more steps, and he leaped the rest of the way.

She lay on her back, only her arms and legs visible beneath the wayward snowman.

Hawkins scooped up Frosty and hastily set him aside

before reaching for Annalise. He pulled her to her feet. "Are you okay?"

"Yeah." The word whooshed out on a breath. "Mr. Snowman there is a little heavier than he looks."

Hawkins bit back a laugh. "Mmm-hmm."

She scowled up at him. "You're laughing at me."

Unable to stifle his amusement, he said, "No, I'm laughing *with* you."

"I wasn't laughing." Her words came out on a chortle.

"You are now."

She gave him a playful shove.

"You're cute when you blush."

Her hands immediately covered her cheeks. "I am not blushing."

No doubt from embarrassment. At least he hoped that was it.

Reeling in his laughter, he closed the distance between them and palmed her elbows. "Seriously, you're not hurt, are you?"

Her expression sobered. "Only my pride."

A small stem of dried pine needles poked out of her hair. He released her and reached for it, savoring the sweet smell of her.

"What—"

He held up the perpetrator. "Must've been on the floor."

Her gaze was riveted to his. "Yeah."

She was so close. One more step and he could—

"Whoa! This place looks so much bigger without the tractor." At the sound of Gloriana's voice, they practically leaped away from each other.

Had his sister seen them? Known they were just a hairbreadth away from kissing? Maybe. It had certainly been on his mind.

If Gloriana suspected anything, she didn't reveal it.

What had he been thinking? And was Annalise having similar thoughts?

"Look at this snowman we found." Somehow Annalise managed to act as though nothing had happened. And for her, perhaps nothing had. But for him…

"I like it. He's got a nice vintage vibe that'll go perfect with the truck." She looked from Annalise to Hawkins and back. "Have you got a minute? I'd like to go over Gary's sketches with you again to make sure the proposed layout will provide optimum results or see if we need to tweak anything."

Annalise nodded. "Sure. That's not a problem."

His sister faced him. "You okay by yourself while we run to the house?"

"Of course." Matter of fact, it was probably just as well that Annalise stepped away for a while. Give him time to regroup. He barely knew Annalise. And while he might not put her in the same category as Bridget, he had no business pursuing anything beyond friendship until he knew more about the pretty single mom.

If you keep comparing every woman to Bridget, you're never going to find the right one.

Maybe. But if he didn't exercise caution, he'd end up the walking wounded once again.

Chapter Eight

Annalise wasn't sure what was worse. That Hawkins had almost kissed her or that she'd wanted him to. Either way, Gloriana's interruption couldn't have come at a better time. And as the two of them made their way to the house, it didn't appear Gloriana had noticed what was going on between Annalise and Hawkins. Unless the way she kept going on about the barn was a cover.

"I can't get over how different it looks without all of that stuff. Once we come up with some type of barrier to separate the check-in area from the utility space, I think we can make it look quite festive."

Annalise slid her hands into her back pockets as they neared the stoop outside the kitchen door. "I vote for lots of tiny lights, colored or white. We could even wrap some around the rafters. Or maybe drape them to create the illusion of a ceiling."

"Oh, I like that." Gloriana's eyes widened. "Then we'll add some red poinsettias and pine boughs, several wreaths." She paused and took a breath. "I can hardly wait to see it."

"Simple, yet festive." Annalise held the screen as Gloriana pushed the door open and stepped inside.

HARLEQUIN®
Reader Service

FREE BOOKS GIVEAWAY

2 FREE ROMANCE BOOKS!

2 FREE SUSPENSE BOOKS!

GET UP TO FOUR FREE BOOKS & TWO FREE GIFTS WORTH OVER $20!

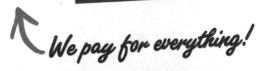

We pay for everything!

See Details Inside

YOU pick your books –
WE pay for everything.
You get up to FOUR New Books and
TWO Mystery Gifts...absolutely FREE!

Dear Reader,

I am writing to announce the launch of a huge **FREE BOOKS GIVEAWAY**... and to let you know that YOU are entitled to choose up to FOUR fantastic books that WE pay for.

Try **Love Inspired® Romance Larger-Print** books and fall in love with inspirational romances that take you on an uplifting journey of faith, forgiveness and hope.

Try **Love Inspired® Suspense Larger-Print** books where courage and optimism unite in stories of faith and love in the face of danger.

Or TRY BOTH!

In return, we ask just one favor: Would you please participate in our brief Reader Survey? We'd love to hear from you.

This FREE BOOKS GIVEAWAY means that your introductory shipment is completely free, <u>even the shipping</u>! If you decide to continue, you can look forward to curated monthly shipments of brand-new books from your selected series, always at a discount off the cover price! <u>Plus you can cancel any time</u>. Who could pass up a deal like that?

Sincerely

Pam Powers

Pam Powers
For Harlequin Reader Service

Complete the survey below and return it today to receive up to 4 FREE BOOKS and FREE GIFTS guaranteed!

▼ DETACH AND MAIL CARD TODAY! ▼

FREE BOOKS GIVEAWAY
Reader Survey

1

Do you prefer books which reflect Christian values?

◯ YES   ◯ NO

2

Do you share your favorite books with friends?

◯ YES   ◯ NO

3

Do you often choose to read instead of watching TV?

◯ YES   ◯ NO

YES! Please send me my Free Rewards, consisting of **2 Free Books from each series I select** and **Free Mystery Gifts**. I understand that I am under no obligation to buy anything, no purchase necessary see terms and conditions for details.

❑ Love Inspired® Romance Larger-Print (122/322 IDL GRQV)
❑ Love Inspired® Suspense Larger-Print (107/307 IDL GRQV)
❑ Try Both (122/322 & 107/307 IDL GRQ7)

FIRST NAME   LAST NAME

ADDRESS

APT.#   CITY

STATE/PROV.   ZIP/POSTAL CODE

EMAIL ❑   Please check this box if you would like to receive newsletters and promotional emails from Harlequin Enterprises ULC and its affiliates. You can unsubscribe anytime.

Your Privacy – Your information is being collected by Harlequin Enterprises ULC, operating as Harlequin Reader Service. For a complete summary of the information we collect, how we use this information and to whom it is disclosed, please visit our privacy notice located at https://corporate.harlequin.com/privacy-notice. From time to time we may also exchange your personal information with reputable third parties. If you wish to opt out of this sharing of your personal information, please visit www.readerservice.com/consumerschoice or call 1-800-873-8635. **Notice to California Residents** – Under California law, you have specific rights to control and access your data. For more information on these rights and how to exercise them, visit https://corporate.harlequin.com/california-privacy.

LI/LIS-122-FBG22_LI/LIS-122-FBGVR

© 2022 HARLEQUIN ENTERPRISES ULC
® and ™ are trademarks owned and used by the trademark owner and/or its licensee. Printed in the U.S.A.

HARLEQUIN® Reader Service — **Terms and Conditions:**

Accepting your 2 free books and 2 free gifts (gifts valued at approximately $10.00 retail) places you under no obligation to buy anything. You may keep the books and gifts and return the shipping statement marked "cancel." If you do not cancel, approximately one month later we'll send you 6 more books from each series you have chosen, and bill you at our low, subscribers-only discount price. Love Inspired® Romance Larger-Print books and Love Inspired® Suspense Larger-Print books consist of 6 books each month and cost just $6.24 each in the U.S. or $6.49 each in Canada. That is a savings of at least 17% off the cover price. It's quite a bargain! Shipping and handling is just 50¢ per book in the U.S. and $1.25 per book in Canada*. You may return any shipment at our expense and cancel at any time by calling the number below — or you may continue to receive monthly shipments at our low, subscribers-only discount price plus shipping and handling. *Terms and prices subject to change without notice. Prices do not include sales taxes which will be charged (if applicable) based on your state or country of residence. Canadian residents will be charged applicable taxes. Offer not valid in Quebec. Books received may not be as shown. All orders subject to approval. Credit or debit balances in a customer's account(s) may be offset by any other outstanding balance owed by or to the customer. Please allow 3 to 4 weeks for delivery. Offer available while quantities last. **Your Privacy** – Your information is being collected by Harlequin Enterprises ULC, operating as Harlequin Reader Service. For a complete summary of the information we collect, how we use this information and to whom it is disclosed, please visit our privacy notice located at https://corporate.harlequin.com/privacy-notice. From time to time we may also exchange your personal information with reputable third parties. If you wish to opt out of this sharing of your personal information, please visit www.readerservice.com/consumerschoice or call 1-800-873-8635. **Notice to California Residents** – Under California law, you have specific rights to control and access your data. For more information on these rights and how to exercise them, visit https://corporate.harlequin.com/california-privacy.

▲ If offer card is missing write to: Harlequin Reader Service, P.O. Box 1341, Buffalo, NY 14240-8531 or visit www.ReaderService.com ▲

BUSINESS REPLY MAIL
FIRST-CLASS MAIL   PERMIT NO. 717   BUFFALO, NY

POSTAGE WILL BE PAID BY ADDRESSEE

HARLEQUIN READER SERVICE
PO BOX 1341
BUFFALO NY 14240-8571

NO POSTAGE
NECESSARY
IF MAILED
IN THE
UNITED STATES

"Can I get you something?" Annalise closed the door behind her. "Coffee? Water? Pumpkin spice muffin?"

"A muffin sounds delicious."

While Annalise washed her hands, Olivia toddled in from the living room, with Francie close behind.

"There's that precious little cherub." Gloriana scooped the child into her arms and kissed her mercilessly until Olivia giggled.

Drying her hands, Annalise still couldn't get over how the entire Prescott family seemed to adore her daughter. And they weren't afraid to show their affection. Quite different from her parents, who oftentimes barely acknowledged Olivia. Unless there was a photo op: then they were suddenly the adoring grandparents.

They just speak a different love language, she reminded herself.

She tossed the towel aside and retrieved the plastic storage container from beside the stove, realizing that the only time she'd even talked with her parents in the two-and-a-half weeks she'd been in Hope Crossing was when she'd called them that first night, letting them know she and Olivia had arrived safely. Though, there had been a couple of texts, both of which were in response to photos she'd sent them of Olivia and the Christmas trees.

"Here you go." She set the muffins on the table before moving to the sideboard. "Let me grab Gary's journals."

"That won't be necessary," said Gloriana.

Her steps slowed as Hawkins' sister continued. "Confession time."

Annalise turned as Gloriana stood Olivia on the floor.

Gripping the back of a chair, the pretty brunette kept her gaze fixed on Annalise. "The layout isn't the only reason I pulled you away from the barn."

Suddenly, Annalise's insides were as tangled as a strand

of Christmas lights. Gloriana must have seen her and Hawkins. Known what likely would've happened had she not spoken up.

Annalise swallowed hard, attempting to dislodge the lump in her throat. She and Hawkins had been spending a lot of time together. It stood to reason his sister would want to protect him. Annalise was a single mother, after all. Widowed, at that. Perhaps they thought she was looking for a man to take care of her and Olivia. Yet while stranger things had happened, she'd need to assure them she wasn't looking for a man, or anyone else, to take care of them.

"We wanted to discuss something with you, dear." Francie's dark eyes seemed to bore into her. Had Gloriana somehow been able to tell her mother what she saw in the barn? Assuming she actually saw them. Did they not want Annalise anywhere near Hawkins?

"O-okay." She needed to pull herself together and assure them that she was not after him. On the contrary, she needed to keep her distance.

"Hawkins' birthday is the first weekend in November," said Gloriana. "He's turning forty, and we're thinking about throwing him a party."

Annalise's thoughts skidded to a halt as she tried to follow what they were saying. "A-a party?"

"With him living in Alaska, it's been years since we've been able to celebrate with him." Francie stooped to pick up Olivia, who'd been clamoring at her feet. "And since it's a milestone birthday, we thought it might be nice to do things up right and include some of his old friends."

Willing her shoulders to relax, she grabbed a muffin from the table, trying to mentally regroup. "Yeah, sounds like a great idea."

"But we want it to be a surprise." Gloriana's eyes glimmered.

The tension slowly began to drain from Annalise. "A surprise party. Got it."

"You're invited, of course." Francie squeezed the child in her arms as she added, "And Olivia."

"We wondered if you might be able to help us, though." Gloriana reached for a muffin and took a bite.

Annalise sucked in a breath, willing all the thoughts from moments ago to disappear so she could concentrate. "Help you how?"

"We need to make sure he's distracted the day of the party."

"Where are you planning to have it?"

"At my and Justin's place."

"Which he drives past anytime he goes to or leaves the cabin, so he'd notice any extra vehicles," said Francie.

"So we kind of need him gone," added Gloriana.

Annalise shifted from one foot to the next. "I mean, I'm sure I could come up with something here for him to help me with, but it would likely involve work, and I don't think he'd want to show up at a party all sweaty and dirty."

"We've already thought of that, dear." Francie's grin held an air of mischief.

"We'd like you to invite him to dinner the night of the party," said Gloriana.

"But wouldn't he be suspicious as to why you all didn't invite him for a birthday dinner?"

"No, because the party is on a Saturday night and his birthday is Sunday."

"Okay, so I invite him to dinner. Do you want me to actually feed him?"

"No. Tell him you're taking him out. Sure, he'll probably balk about that not being fair to you, but I know you'll be able to come up with some excuse. Then, you offer to drive. Tell him you don't want to move Olivia's car seat or something like that."

Annalise felt her brows lift. "So you want me to drive him to your place?"

"That's right. Except, he'll be blindfolded."

Unable to stop herself, Annalise burst out laughing. "You two seriously think he's going to agree to that?"

"It may take a little coaxing," said Francie. "Just tell him you want to surprise him. He'll do it for you."

Annalise sobered. "And how do you know that?"

"Because you're a lovely young woman and he enjoys your company," said Francie.

"You make him smile," added Gloriana. "Worst case, you weaponize Olivia."

"What does that mean?"

"In case you haven't noticed, she's got him wrapped around her tiny little finger." Gloriana pretended to nibble the child's hand. "Not to mention, the rest of us."

They were right about that. Hawkins definitely had a soft spot where her daughter was concerned. All the way back to that day at Plowman's.

Then Annalise thought about what had happened just now in the barn. Was Hawkins interested in something more than friendship with her? Or did his interest have more to do with her daughter? What if he saw himself as a knight in shining armor? The kind of guy who liked to swoop in and save the day or was partial to grand gestures the way Dylan had been. Gestures that had bolstered his ego but left her longing for his acceptance and love.

She squared her shoulders. She and Olivia weren't in need of a hero. They deserved better. They deserved someone who would be there through good times and bad. Someone who would not only shelter them from life's storms but ride them out with them, holding them tightly. Someone whose love for her she'd never doubt.

No, she'd been in one loveless marriage. She'd rather spend her life alone than go through that ever again.

Something wasn't right.

Standing in the living room of the cabin late the following Wednesday morning, Hawkins watched through the window as a ten-point buck ambled into the woods and the wind whipped the trees into another frenzy. Ever since that almost-kiss in the barn a week ago, Annalise had been avoiding him.

When she'd finally rejoined him after going off with his sister, she'd seemed...different. Her playfulness that had made the work seem less like a chore had evaporated. Instead, she worked without saying much at all until the barn had been transformed from a giant catchall to an organized workspace on one end while leaving plenty of room near the front for a welcome center and the sale of things like wreaths, garlands and tree stands.

Thursday and Friday he and Annalise tackled the smaller shed, unpacking all of the boxes and moving their contents to wherever they'd be needed. Again with little chitchat, only Christmas music filling the air between them.

Tom, who'd managed to knock out a good majority of the trees that would make up this year's inventory, had pointed out some items they hadn't been aware of, such as a large *Christmas Tree Farm* banner along with some other signs and dozens of ten-foot PVC pipes that had been hidden along the overgrown backside of the barn. Tom said they were to serve as measuring sticks, aiding shoppers in their quest for the right tree.

And through it all, Annalise kept her distance. Both physically and emotionally. Not at all like the woman who'd seemed to enjoy working with him prior to her little mishap with Frosty. Had Gloriana's sudden appearance completely embarrassed her? Or did the notion of kissing Hawkins repel her that much?

Now, with the grunt work out of the way, she no longer needed his help. Annalise, Mom and Gloriana could handle the setup and decorations by themselves. And here he was, three days into his new position, working with a great group of engineers on an offshore project that should excite him, yet feeling absolutely miserable.

Annalise obviously had no use for him anymore. And as much as he hated to admit, it stung. He'd foolishly thought something was growing between them. Obviously, he was wrong. Not for the first time.

One hand shoved in the pocket of his jeans, he turned from the window and crossed the wood floor to the kitchen. After refilling his coffee mug, he continued to the desk behind the couch where he eyed the blueprint on his laptop screen. *Come on, Hawk. Get your head in the game.*

His phone buzzed, and he hated the way his hopes soared when he saw Annalise's name on the screen.

"Hello?"

"I have a problem." Her breathless tone had him ready to head for his truck.

But he willed himself to stay put. "What is it?"

"Olivia and I went to the barn to get something, and the wind caught one of the doors and pulled it off one of its hinges. Now it's just kind of hanging there, while the wind tosses it back and forth. I about jumped out of my skin when it crashed into the barn."

"Are you and Olivia okay?"

"Yes, although I'm afraid that if we don't get it fixed, we're going to lose the door completely."

He closed out his computer. "I'm on my way."

After double-checking the toolbox in the bed of his truck to make sure he had what he'd need for the repair, he hopped into the cab and sped up the drive. Then forced himself to slow down when he recalled how miserable he'd been before Annalise's call. She was the one who'd erected the wall between them, and yet he was ready to drop everything and come to her rescue at the first sign of trouble. Just the way he had with Bridget.

She has a kid. Besides, you have an interest in the tree farm, too.

Whatever.

Annalise came out of the house with Olivia on her hip as he brought his truck to a stop alongside the barn a short time later.

He stepped out and rounded the corner of the building as another wind gust caught the door dangling precariously by its lower hinge and sent it sailing toward him. He dodged out of the way and managed to grab hold of it before it hit the barn.

"This wind is wicked."

He turned at Annalise's voice. While her hair was held captive in a ponytail, little Olivia's was at the mercy of the wind. Not that she had all that much.

"I made sure the other door was latched on the inside," she said.

"Good." Keeping a hand on the damaged door, he eased toward the structure to study the old iron hinges. "I'm going to need your help." He faced Annalise. "Any thoughts on where we could put Olivia so she'll be safe?"

She observed the clouds racing across the sky, playing peekaboo with the sun. "I could put her high chair in the barn and ply her with food."

"With all this dust flying around? It's not like the barn is insulated."

With a sigh, she glanced toward the house. "The only other thing I can think of is to pull my car down here and put her in her car seat. She won't like it, but she'll be safe."

Hawkins moved to the other end of the door to look inside the barn. Eyeing the boxes they'd brought over from the shed, he said, "I have an idea."

He hurried inside to a group of boxes along the opposite wall and began emptying a very large square one that was almost as tall as Olivia. Once empty, he returned to where Annalise and her daughter now stood just inside the door and set it on the dirt floor. "Kids love boxes. How about we let her play in this?"

Nodding, Annalise peered up at him. "She'll need some toys."

He tugged his keys from his pocket, removed the fob and handed them to Olivia.

Wearing a goofy grin, she snatched them, then held them up to her mother as if to say, *Look what I got.*

"What about my phone?" He removed it from his pocket. "Does she watch videos?"

"She's a little too young for that. I'll run up to the house and grab a few things."

He contemplated offering to keep Olivia with him but thought better of it. Instead, he used the time to evaluate the hinge, which was bent but still usable, and formulate a plan.

After locating some blocks of wood he'd come across during their barn cleanup, not to mention bolts, washers and nuts, he retrieved a socket set and crescent wrench from his truck as Annalise rejoined him.

Once Olivia was jabbering happily in her box, Hawkins grabbed two full gas cans.

Arms crossed over her chest, Annalise sent him a curious look. "What do you need gas for?"

"Nothing. But they're heavy." He nodded toward the latched door. "Open this for me, please."

Though she did as he asked, she said, "I thought you said it was good that I'd latched it."

"It was." Against the wind, he pushed the door to a forty-five-degree angle with his shoulder, then set a gas can on either side of it to hopefully hold it in place.

Straightening, he moved to the other door, which stood halfway open, swaying ever so slightly. "We're going to have to close this to reattach the hinge. Once I get the bolts in place, you'll go inside and add the washers and nuts to secure the bolts.

"Got it."

Between the wind and the strained bottom hinge, he struggled but finally managed to close the door before shifting his focus to Annalise. "I need you to help me lift this door enough to align the holes in the hinge with the holes in the barn."

Annalise's brow puckered as the wind lifted her ponytail. "I'm not sure I'll be able to hold it. It isn't exactly light."

"That's why I have these." He retrieved the wood blocks from inside. "I'll tuck them underneath the door as an assist." He laid them out on the dirt, as close to the door as possible. "Are you ready?" He gripped the horizontal brace.

With a nod, Annalise did, too.

"Okay, go." As they lifted, he nudged a couple of the

two-by-four pieces under the door with the toe of his boot. Then he checked the proximity of the hinge to the holes.

"Need to go a little higher." He picked up two more blocks and handed them to her. "When I lift the door, you position these on top of the ones that are already there."

She did as he asked, and it was just enough to put the hinge at the proper height.

"I'll need to coax this hinge into place with a hammer, so I want you to hold the door steady as best you can."

She nodded and a short time later he was threading the bolts through the holes.

"Okay." Winded, he reached into his pocket and pulled out the washers and nuts. "While I keep things steady out here, you to go inside and add a washer first, then a nut to each bolt."

"I'm not sure I'll be able to reach."

He eyed the height of the hinge before lowering his gaze to her. "Use the ladder."

He heard Olivia whimper as her mother worked to get the ladder in place. Minutes later, while he continued to hold each bolt in position, Annalise did as he'd instructed on the other side of the wall. All the while, Olivia grew fussier.

"Okay, I'm done," Annalise said much sooner than he'd anticipated.

By the time he joined her inside, she was holding a still crying Olivia and inching toward the door.

"She's ready for lunch and a nap," she said.

He continued to where she'd been working. "Just let me check these before you go." Stepping on the first rung of the ladder, he eyed the bolts. The nuts were barely sitting on the end of each. Why hadn't she tightened them? "Hey, hold up, Annalise."

When she didn't respond, he glanced toward the door to discover she was gone.

As he stepped off the ladder to go after her, another gust had the door straining. And before he could make it outside to hold it in place, the hinged yanked free.

A guttural groan escaped his lips as frustration burned inside him. *"Annalise!"* He glanced toward the house as she closed the door behind her. What was she doing? He'd told her wait.

The temptation to leave was almost overwhelming. But he knew he'd regret it later. And while he really wanted to march up to the house and tell her to get back out here and help him, Olivia would be a problem.

As he wrestled the door into place, all the while hoping there would be no more big gusts until the task was completed, he chastised himself for again falling prey to a woman whose only interest in him was what he could do for her. Oh, he'd tried to convince himself that Annalise was different, that she wasn't anything like Bridget. Obviously he was delusional.

When he finally had the hinge in alignment, he shoved one bolt through, then rushed inside the barn to secure it. Then he repeated the process with the other two bolts, his irritation mounting each and every step of the way. He got that Annalise needed his help. She had her daughter to think about. But to blatantly walk away and expect him to finish the job *she* needed him to do?

Once everything was secure, he gathered up his tools and was about to step out of the barn when his phone rang. He looked at the screen half expecting it to be Annalise. Instead, it was his boss.

"Yes, sir?"

"Hawkins, I was just checking in to see if you had a

chance to look over the blueprints. I'd halfway expected to hear from you by now."

He would have if Annalise hadn't bailed on him. "I have one more thing to check over, but I'll get back to you within the hour."

"Sounds good."

Determined to keep that promise, he hastily secured both doors on the barn, stowed his tools in the bed of his truck and was about to hop into the cab when Annalise came running toward him.

"I just got Olivia down for her nap. I didn't realize you were still here. Was there a problem?"

"I told you to wait until I made sure the bolts were secure."

"But—"

"Instead, you used Olivia as an excuse to run off, leaving me to redo things by myself after the wind yanked out the bolts *you* failed to secure."

"Oh, no. I'm—"

"Let's get something straight. I am not your beck-and-call boy. You don't get to call me over here and then run off and expect me to do something by myself."

"What? But I didn't. I just assumed—"

"We agreed to collaborate. That means we both do our share of the work. But I will *not* allow you to take advantage of me."

With that, he threw himself into the cab, fired up the engine and sped away.

Chapter Nine

Annalise stormed back into her house. How dare Hawkins accuse her of using him. Especially after she'd worked every bit as hard as he had last week. She'd enjoyed herself, too. Right up until that almost-kiss when Gloriana had interrupted them and then stolen her away so she and Francie could pull Annalise into their covert plans for Hawkins' birthday.

Hands on her hips, she huffed out a breath. She needed to bake something. Baking always calmed her.

Her gaze drifted to the bunch of black bananas sitting on the counter. Seconds later, she was gathering the rest of the ingredients for banana nut bread, along with three small loaf pans that would allow her to indulge in one loaf now while the other two could go into the freezer for another day.

After mashing the bananas, she set the oven to preheat, then added the butter and sugar to the bowl of her stand mixer, set it to medium and turned it on. Thinking back on the conversation she'd had with Hawkins' mother and sister in this very room, she recalled that moment when her euphoria brought on by the look in Hawkins' eyes had morphed into fear, drawing her into an imaginary world where he was just like Dylan.

She added the eggs, one at a time, asking herself why she'd fallen for Dylan in the first place. And as she spooned in some sour cream, she knew it had been his confidence that had drawn her to him. She'd always been insecure and liked his outgoing manner. He was a take-charge kind of guy. Not to mention charming.

Turning off the mixer, she combined her dry ingredients in a separate bowl. It wasn't until after Dylan died that she realized he'd had his fair share of insecurities, too. His dad had walked out on a six-year-old Dylan and his mother to marry his pregnant girlfriend. A woman whose family had money. According to Dylan, he never saw his father much after that, and his mother had bounced from one man to the next, hoping one of them would be a father to Dylan. Meanwhile, Dylan pushed himself to be the best at whatever he did—sports, school, work—all the while hoping his father would take notice of him.

She turned the mixer on low and added the flour mixture a little at a time, realizing Dylan's tendencies had carried into their marriage, as well. He excelled at his job. Pushed himself to be the best. Nice house, nice car. Toward the end, he'd even started buying clothes for Annalise because the stuff she'd picked out wasn't stylish enough.

By the time she'd stirred in the bananas and was spooning the batter into the pans, she couldn't help wondering if all that pressure he'd put on himself had sent him to an early grave. No one should be that consumed with trying to impress others. Especially when they were created by a God who loved them just the way they were, who sent

His one and only Son to die for them and longed to have a relationship with them.

Yet while Annalise had come to that realization, Dylan had merely gone through the motions, attending church at Christmas and Easter, decked out in one of his custom-tailored suits with the matching silk tie and pocket square while he pretended his life was perfect.

A tear trailed down her cheek as she placed the pans into the hot oven. She'd wanted to be enough for Dylan. To be the one to heal all those wounds from his past. But he was too busy playing the hero to even consider that he might need one, too.

She set the timer before moving the dirty dishes into the sink and turning on the water. Hawkins was nothing like Dylan. He didn't pretend to be someone he wasn't. And he'd never tried to change her. He wasn't afraid to let her take the lead and was always there to encourage her whenever she doubted herself. And as for Olivia, there was no hiding the fact that he adored her. But that look in his eyes when he'd almost kissed Annalise had nothing to do with her daughter. It was pure attraction. And that scared her because she'd felt it, too.

So what should she do now?

She eyed the water as it overflowed from the bowl into the sink. Turning off the faucet, she knew she owed him an apology. Not only for what had happened with the barn but for her behavior this past week. And as soon as Olivia woke from her nap and the bread was out of the oven, she'd do just that.

Yet as she carried Olivia into the kitchen shortly after the bread finished baking, there was a knock at her door.

"Who do you suppose that is, baby?" Maybe Hawkins had returned. Then again, as angry as he'd been, she didn't see that happening.

She opened the door.

"Annalise!" MaryAnn Adams, Annalise's mother, pulled the screen door wide and stepped inside wearing a flowing black tunic-style shirt, khaki-colored capris and pointed black ballet flats. "How are my babies?" She embraced both Annalise and Olivia with her usual fanfare.

"We're good." Annalise's gaze drifted to her father, who stood nearby, hands in the pockets of his stone-colored golf pants. "A little surprised, at the moment."

When her mother released her, her dad stepped forward, wearing a maroon polo shirt that bore the Adams Realty logo.

A moment later, Annalise looked from one parent to the next. "What are you doing here? And why didn't you tell me you were coming?"

"We wanted to surprise you." Mom finger-combed her ash-blond layered bob with perfectly manicured nails, her sizable diamond ring catching the light.

"We also have some news you might find interesting." Dad's smile reached his indigo eyes that were so like her own.

"Oh?" Annalise couldn't imagine.

Her mother clasped her hands together, the multiple bracelets on her wrists tinkling. Yet she showed no interest in holding her granddaughter. "We've been doing some research into your property here."

"Why?" Lifting a brow, she shifted Olivia to her other arm.

"Somebody has to look out for your best interest," said Dad. "We discovered you're sitting on quite a gold mine."

Mom's smile grew wider. "Properties like yours are wildly popular with well-to-do people in both Houston and Austin. They're looking for an escape and are willing to pay top dollar for it."

Annalise's gaze darted between them. "But I don't want to sell."

"Sweetheart, with fifteen acres, we're talking over a million dollars, easy. Even more if we can get a bidding war going. You could live anywhere you want." Her mother's blue-gray eyes skimmed the cozy living room. "Have a bigger house."

"I don't want or need a bigger house." Annalise started toward the kitchen. "Follow me. I want to show you my Christmas tree farm." She slipped her bare feet into her sneakers by the kitchen door before heading outside.

The winds had calmed some and the clouds had vanished, allowing the sun to warm the afternoon air to a comfortable eighty degrees.

Her excitement grew as she continued into the garage. Once her parents saw all the trees and she laid out her vision for future growth, they might finally understand why she wanted to stay here. They might even be proud of her entrepreneurial spirit, something they'd always admired in others.

She paused beside the utility vehicle. "Hop in."

While her father cast an admiring grin at the machine, her mother's perfectly arched brows rose.

"Are you sure it's safe?"

"Olivia and I ride in it all the time." They'd gotten into a habit of making a drive through the trees every evening. Something that seemed to relax both of them, not to mention keep Annalise apprised of anything that might need attention.

A short time later, they were traversing the rows of Virginia pines while Annalise explained the difference between them and the Leyland cypresses. Mom sat in the middle, awkwardly holding Olivia, while Dad studied things from the passenger seat.

"I did hit one little snag when I first arrived." Annalise went on to explain about the land Gary had taken from the Prescotts. "But God worked everything out. We decided to collaborate, which has been a real blessing. Hawkins helped with the heavy lifting, while his sister, Gloriana, has been establishing a website and coming up with promotional ideas I never would've considered. She worked in television for years, so she knows how to spread the word." She let go a sigh. "And then their mother, Francie, has watched Olivia countless times so I could help Hawkins."

"That's good that you've had help, but how do you know you can trust these people?" Her mother's gaze bore into her as they again neared the garage.

"Because they've gone out of their way to help me, almost from the minute I arrived. And they've never expected anything in return."

While Mom didn't respond, she cast a knowing look to her husband, but he was too busy engaging with Olivia to notice.

Annalise eased the utility vehicle between the barn and the little red shed, eager to show them the barn and her plans for the welcome center. As she turned off the engine, though, she heard someone coming up the drive.

Stepping onto the gravel, she moved to the corner of the barn as Hawkins' truck appeared.

A sinking feeling pulled at her stomach. Why was he back? Had he forgotten something? Or was he still angry and had returned to give her another piece of his mind?

You wanted to talk to him.

That was before her parents showed up. Not that she didn't want to apologize, just not in front of them.

"Who is that?" Her mother was beside her now, her tone laced with skepticism.

Despite her own wariness, Annalise put one foot in front of the other and met him as he got out of his truck. "I wasn't expecting to see you so soon."

His expression gave nothing away as to his reason for being there. "I need to…" His dark gaze drifted to her parents. Even though he didn't know who they were.

"Come meet my parents."

Olivia toddled toward them as they rejoined her folks.

Lifting her daughter into her arms, Annalise said, "Mom, Dad, this is Hawkins Prescott." She glanced up at him. "These are my parents, Paul and MaryAnn Adams."

"Pleased to meet you." He shook her father's hand first before doing the same with her mother.

While her father smiled, Mom gave him a once-over with wary eyes.

"Awk!" Olivia clapped her hands.

Facing her daughter, he said, "I didn't forget you, little one." He tugged his cap off and placed it on her head.

Olivia tee-heed before removing it and passing it back to him.

"I was showing my parents around the farm."

"It looks a lot different than when she first arrived." Hawkins' smile *seemed* sincere. "Annalise has put in a lot of hard work to get things ready. Before long, this place will be crawling with people in search of the perfect Christmas tree."

Mom fingered her long silver-tassel necklace. "Yes, a fun *holiday* event, but what about the rest of the year?"

Annalise stared at her mother, trying to quell her frustration. "It's not like the tree farm is my only source of income. I'm still with Heart and Soul Ministries." She toed at the dirt. "That said, I would like to grow this place into something more than just Christmas. I'm toying with the idea of expanding things to include a pumpkin farm in the fall. Maybe add a plant nursery in the spring or a farmers' market.

"Way out here?" Her mother laughed at the notion, discounting Annalise's dreams the way she'd always done.

Dad did, too. And while their reaction was all too familiar, it still stung.

"You'd be surprised," Hawkins said. "If you're offering something people want, they're willing to drive just about any distance to get it." He glanced at Annalise. And although it was brief, the look in his eyes, the unexpected warmth, said far more than his words. "Your daughter has a good mind for business and a heart for people. She's also got some outstanding ideas. I think her Christmas tree farm is not only going to be a huge success, but that she's going to surprise us all."

If Annalise had questioned her feelings for Hawkins prior to this moment, her doubts had been eradicated right then and there. No one had ever believed in her the way he seemed to. Making him impossible to resist.

Hawkins poured a cup of coffee in his cabin late the next morning, kicking himself for behaving like such a jerk. He had no business jumping all over Annalise yesterday. Yes, he'd been frustrated when the hinge came undone, and even more so when his boss called, but comparing her to Bridget and then taking his anger out on Annalise was wrong on so many levels.

He needed to apologize in a big way. Just not in front of her parents. The way they'd laughed at Annalise's ideas still rubbed him the wrong way. Did they not recognize the courage it took for her to pull up stakes and move her and her daughter from Dallas to Hope Crossing to start a new life? Could they not see her passion for what she was doing and her plans for the future?

Or did they purposely choose to ignore it?

He recalled that day he'd driven Annalise to Brenham to pick up a new battery. Though he'd been skeptical at the time, Annalise was right. Her parents did see her as incapable.

Taking a sip of the steaming brew, he contemplated the determined woman he'd worked alongside for nearly a month now. Annalise might have been a fish out of water when she'd arrived in Hope Crossing, but she'd worked hard not only to acclimate but to establish the foundation for what she hoped would be a legacy for her daughter. And that fascinated him more than he dared admit.

Still, the pain and embarrassment Bridget had caused him lingered.

For the gazillionth time, Annalise is not Bridget!

No, she was not. Annalise's strength of character and kind heart were things Bridget never possessed. Making him wonder why he'd ever been interested in her in the first place.

Shoving a hand through his hair, he returned to his computer. No doubt about it, he needed to talk with Annalise and soon. Maybe he should text her, find out when her parents were leaving.

He'd just picked up his phone when there was a knock at the door. Still holding his coffee mug, he crossed the room, tucking the phone in his pocket as he went. Excitement tangled with trepidation when hc opened the door to find Annalise holding her daughter.

"Awk." Olivia's grin sparkled in her blue eyes.

His smile was as instantaneous as it was tremulous. "Hey, there, sunshine." His gaze drifted to her mother. "This is quite a surprise." Then again, after the way he'd behaved yesterday, perhaps Annalise was eager to give him a piece of her mind.

"We would have come by sooner, but my parents only left an hour ago." She held out a foil-wrapped package. "This is for you. Homemade banana nut bread."

"Sounds good." He accepted it, then stepped aside, motioning for them to come inside. "Did you enjoy your time with your folks?"

"Not particularly." She faced him as he closed the door. "They were here on a mission."

"What sort of mission?"

"They want me to sell the Christmas tree farm."

The thought of her leaving had his gut tightening.

"They kept going on and on about how much money I'd stand to make so I could get a bigger and better house."

"What's wrong with your house? It's cute. And it's only you and Olivia."

"That's what I told them." She huffed out a breath. "Look, I didn't come here to talk about my parents, thereby sending my blood pressure through the roof."

Though he chuckled, he suddenly needed some space. He crossed to the counter that separated the kitchen and living area and set down his cup and the bread. "Then, why did you come?"

He could feel her watching him while she stood there, just inside the door, seemingly frozen. As if she was waiting for permission to advance. "To apologize."

He whirled to face her, certain he'd misunderstood. "For what?"

"For abandoning you at the barn yesterday. While it's true that I did not hear you when you told me to wait until you checked the bolts, I was also eager to leave."

"Because?"

"All week, I've purposely been keeping my distance from you." She stood a squirming Olivia on the wooden floor. "Ever since that day we cleared out the barn."

The day everything had been going great. Until they'd almost kissed. Annalise had behaved differently ever since.

He watched Olivia toddle toward him, then lifted her into his arms. "Because of what almost happened?"

"Because I allowed my mind to wander down a path it shouldn't have, and let my insecurities get the best of me."

He finally met her gaze. "So why are you here now?"

"Because you stood up for me." She took a step closer. "Hawkins, you have believed in me even when I haven't. No one has ever done that before."

He swallowed around something in his throat. "Then, they were the fools. And so was I. I'm sorry I yelled at you yesterday. I guess we're both guilty of being afraid of our mistakes."

"What do you mean? What did you do?"

He motioned toward the living area. "Why don't we sit down?"

While she took a seat on the sofa, he settled into the recliner beside it with Olivia. "The last year or so I was in Alaska, I was seeing a woman. Her name was Bridget. She worked at a restaurant I frequented, and we engaged in several conversations before I finally asked her out. Things moved pretty slowly for the first month or so, then she started calling more, asking to see me. Honestly, I was flattered. And that blinded me to what was really going on."

"Which was?"

"One day she came by and was very upset. Her mother, who lived in Florida, had been diagnosed with cancer. Bridget wanted to visit her, but she couldn't afford the plane ticket. So I offered to cover her expenses."

"Of course you did. That's the kind of guy you are."

He puffed out a laugh, shaking his head. "Just wait.

It gets better." He sucked in a breath. Let it out. "Over the next several months I gave her more money for plane tickets, hotels, medicines her mother couldn't afford."

"That sounds like a lot of money."

"It was." He stood a squirming Olivia on the floor, watching as she reached for the television remote on the old oak coffee table, and her mother gently pried it from her tiny hand, while he sifted through the embarrassing memories in his mind.

"One night while Bridget was again off to see her mother, one of her coworkers approached me. Said she needed to talk to me. Since it was late and the place was virtually empty, she slid into the booth on the opposite side of my table and proceeded to inform me that Bridget had been playing me. Her mother wasn't sick. Nor did she live in Florida. She lived on one of Alaska's remote islands."

Annalise looked at him, her face morphing from disbelief to horror. "How could someone lie like that?"

He held up a hand. "There's more. Bridget was using the money to take trips with some other guy."

Annalise's jaw dropped, and her eyes went wide. "You have got to be kidding me. That's terrible. Horrible. *Downright disgusting.*" Her last two words sounded more like a growl.

"The only thing worse is that I'm guilty of comparing you to her. That's why I lashed out at you yesterday. I had no right to do that. And I'm sorry."

"Apology accepted. Though, totally unnecessary, given my behavior."

He leaned forward. "I can promise you, I won't make that mistake ever again."

She smiled. "Good."

For the next few minutes, silence filled the space between them, save for Olivia's jabbering. Perhaps they were simply processing, but things felt suddenly awkward. Where did they go from here? He'd thought about asking them to accompany him to the church's fall festival this Saturday, but maybe it was too soon. Perhaps he should just ask if she needed any help at her place. He looked her way.

"Is—"

"Would—"

They both chuckled.

He stood. "After all we've been through, why are we suddenly acting so weird?" He moved around the coffee table to grab Olivia.

"Because we just bared our souls." Annalise stood, lifting her gaze to his. "Would you care to join us for dinner tonight?"

He couldn't help smiling. "What have you got planned?"

"I don't know yet."

"In that case, I've got a couple of New York strips thawing in the fridge."

"Ooo… And I've got a fresh bag of russets, some sour cream, cheese and bacon bits. Not to mention salad fixin's."

He stared down at her, feeling as though a weight had been lifted from his shoulders. "Sounds like a meal to me."

"An exceptional one at that."

"Do you have a grill?"

"Yes." She wrinkled her nose. "But I haven't filled my propane tank yet."

"I'll bring one."

"Great." Her smile had a teasing lilt to it. "Maybe I'll even whip up something decadent for dessert."

He was certain his smile mirrored hers. "Sounds like a date to me."

"I can't wait."

Chapter Ten

Hawkins stood among the Christmas trees the first Saturday of November, knowing things had changed since that day at his cabin two weeks ago. More than Annalise returning to work and Olivia starting day care. More than adjusting to a new routine that, more often than not, included the three of them gathering for supper, occasionally with him preparing the meal.

Their friendship had most definitely grown. As though opening up about Bridget had brought down some invisible barrier between them. They were more comfortable with each other, despite the underlying attraction they'd both held at bay.

If he had known that revealing what happened in Alaska would bring them closer, he might have opened up sooner. Because while Annalise had been forthcoming about her feelings of inadequacy and how her husband had deceived her, Hawkins had kept his hurt and embarrassment to himself, fearful of what she might think. Never considering that she'd also experienced the pain of deception.

Now as he held a red, shatterproof ornament, trying to coax Olivia into taking the snowflake-adorned orb and hanging it on the tree so Annalise could get the photo she wanted for her Christmas cards, he eagerly anticipated the evening that lay ahead. Though his birthday wasn't until tomorrow, she was taking him to dinner tonight. That in itself had his hopes soaring. Now he prayed they might have an opportunity to discuss their relationship. Where it might be headed or where they—she—wanted it to go. Sure, he was finding it more difficult to keep his heart in check, but one question remained. Did Annalise feel the same way?

Under a crystal-blue sky, he again waggled the ornament in his hand. "Lookie here, Olivia."

With temps in the eighties, the red sweater dress and cowboy boots she wore might be a little much, but the child had yet to complain.

"Go ahead, baby. You can do it." Annalise stood a few feet away, camera at the ready. "Hang the ball on the tree."

He demonstrated once more before looping the ribbon over his index finger, allowing the ornament to spin as it dangled.

Finally, the child gave a cheeky grin and snatched the decoration from him.

He hurried out of the way, while Annalise snapped shot after shot as Olivia inched toward the Virginia pine and attempted to hang the ornament from one of its limbs.

"Yes!" Annalise's gleeful voice sifted through the air a few moments later as she stared at the camera's screen. "This is perfect." She turned the Nikon so he could see the screen, then flipped through the last series of images.

"Those are great." He looked at the woman who seemed to have softened his hardened heart. "But you're going to have a hard time narrowing it down to just one."

"Baw." Olivia held her little hand up to show him the ornament.

"That's right." He lifted her into his arms. "Ball."

Annalise checked her watch. "We should get going. I need to change Olivia before we head out."

He followed her as she started toward the house. "You still haven't said where we're going." He'd heard about a new upscale restaurant in a neighboring town. Maybe she was taking him there.

"That's because it's a surprise." She eyed him over her shoulder. "So stop asking."

He followed her into the house and waited in the kitchen while she tended to Olivia. Standing beside the wood table, he eyed her to-do list for the Christmas tree farm. A little more than a week ago, the barn had been decorated, both inside and out, so Gloriana could take some photos for a promotional video that had begun running on various social-media platforms on the first day of November. She also had a couple of radio spots lined up closer to the opening, not to mention ads in all the small-town newspapers around the area.

Based on what he'd been hearing, the entire town was excited about the Christmas tree farm. Plowman's had approached Annalise about selling some of their baked goods, while a gift shop had inquired about offering some Christmas decor.

All the while, Hawkins was determined that Annalise and Olivia would have a little fun. He'd driven them around his family's ranch a couple of weeks ago. He smiled now, recalling the look of wonder on Olivia's face as she took in all the cattle.

Last Saturday, they'd gone to the church's fall festival where even more discoveries awaited Annalise's daughter. He'd held on to and walked alongside Olivia on the pony ride. Though, she wasn't too pleased when the ride was over. At least the lollipop tree provided a nice distraction.

He was still smiling when Annalise breezed into the kitchen with her daughter on her hip, looking beyond beautiful in a blue floral jumpsuit that matched her eyes. "Okay, we're ready to go."

Pulling the kitchen door closed behind them, Hawkins said, "I didn't think to move Olivia's car seat to the truck while I was waiting." He'd been too busy reminiscing.

"Not a problem." Annalise continued to her SUV with Olivia. "I'm driving."

"Okaaay." Then again, she had asked him out.

Hands tucked in the pockets of his dark-wash jeans, he stood awkwardly beside the passenger door as she buckled Olivia into her seat.

"Hop in," Annalise said as she emerged and tossed the door closed.

He complied, curious about that mischievous glimmer in her eyes.

After easing behind the wheel, she started the engine. "Oh, since this is a surprise, I'd like you to wear this." Cool air rushed from the vents as she tugged a red bandanna from her bag.

He looked from it to her and back again. "You mean, like, around my neck." Paired with his maroon buttondown, he'd look like a dime-store cowboy.

"No, silly. It's a blindfold."

He felt his eyes widen. "Uh-uh. No way."

"Aw, come on, Hawkins. Play along. I want this to be a surprise."

"I'm a grown man."

"We're never too old for surprises."

He lifted a brow. "Did you just call me old?"

"You're being ridiculous. Forty is not old."

"And that's not until tomorrow."

She dangled the bandanna in front of him. "Just humor me. Please?"

After a long moment, he said, "Oh, all right." Unable to resist, he added, "But only for you."

The pink that tinged her cheeks as she moved to help him tie it gave him a small amount of satisfaction. Not to mention encouragement.

Moments later, she pulled out of the drive and turned right instead of the left they usually took when headed to Prescott Farms. And while he mentally tried to plot their route, hoping to determine where they were going, after twenty-five minutes of twists and turns, he was lost.

"Thank you for helping me with the pictures," she said.

"My pleasure." He smiled, thinking about Olivia's grin. "It was a good day to be outside."

"I heard it's supposed to turn colder tomorrow."

"Yeah, they're calling for another front sometime tonight."

"When?"

"Well, if I wasn't blindfolded, I'd check my phone and give you the exact timing, but sometime after sunset."

"Oh." That little word seemed to hold a great amount of concern.

"Is there a problem?"

"No. I was just…afraid I might have left one of my windows open. That's all."

At the sound of gravel beneath their tires, he said, "Given that we're now on a dirt road, this place must be in the middle of nowhere."

"It's a little off the beaten path."

The vehicle slowed.

"Are we there yet?"

"Just about," she said.

When they finally came to a stop, she turned off the engine and said, "Don't you dare remove that blindfold until I tell you it's okay."

"If you say so." He heard her unbuckle her seat belt.

"And no peeking either."

"You're starting to sound like my bossy sister." He caught the aroma of smoked meat when she opened her door, and his stomach growled. Barbecue was his favorite meal. One he'd missed during his time in Alaska. Yeah, there were a couple of restaurants who made the attempt, but it was never quite right.

The door behind him opened, indicating Annalise was retrieving her daughter. Moments later, the rear door closed and his opened.

Annalise's warm hand touched his. "You can get out now."

Holding her hand, he stepped from the vehicle, feeling a little foolish with the bandanna. He sure hoped she wasn't going to make him wear it into the restaurant.

She inched him over until he heard his door close. Then she turned him ever so slightly.

"Okay, you can take off the blindfold." No need to tell him twice.

He tugged it over his head.

"Surprise!"

The myriad voices had his eyes widening.

While Annalise beamed beside him, he took in the group of people standing in front of the white, painted-brick house he'd grown up in that now belonged to his sister and brother-in-law. His stepfather, Bill, Justin, Kyleigh, most everyone from their Sunday school class, some with their kids, stood in front of him.

"Happy birthday, Hawkins." His mother approached, wrapped her arms around his waist and gave him a squeeze.

Gloriana was right behind her. "Judging by the look on your face, I believe we succeeded in surprising you." She gave him a one-armed hug. "Thanks to Annalise."

His gaze drifted to hers. "So this is why you insisted on driving."

She shrugged. "You of all people know how hard it is to say no to these two."

Yes, he did. And as he glimpsed the storm clouds building to the north, he found himself questioning Annalise's motivations.

Forcing a smile, he again looked at his friends and family, trying not to let disappointment quell his euphoria. Problem was, he'd been looking forward to spending tonight with Annalise. Eager to find out if she saw him as just a friend or something more. Yet while she'd seemed excited about the prospect, too, she had known what was waiting at the end of their drive. Now he couldn't help wondering if her excitement had been purely about the event rather than being with him.

"That storm was scary." Sitting in the passenger seat of her SUV with only the glow of the dashboard for light, Annalise rubbed her arms, trying to warm herself while Hawkins drove them home. His party—which had taken place in Gloriana's backyard where patio lights illuminated the space while they'd feasted on good old Texas barbecue, played numerous rounds of cornhole and enjoyed the company of friends—seemed to be a success, despite the storm that had shut things down a little earlier than anticipated.

Hawkins had barely finished unwrapping his gifts when lightning streaked across the night sky accompanied by some of the loudest thunder she'd ever heard. Soon, everyone's phones were blowing up with significant-weather advisories proclaiming the possibility of hail and winds in excess of fifty miles per hour.

So while guests rushed home and Kyleigh watched over Olivia inside Gloriana's house, Annalise helped the family bring in the food and secure anything that could possibly turn into a projectile. Then they rode out the fast-moving storm's driving rain and winds reminiscent of *The Wizard of Oz* in the hallway of the house, just to be safe.

"That's a norther for you."

"You mean like a blue norther?"

"Yep." Both hands on the steering wheel, he stared straight ahead. "Tomorrow we'll all need jackets."

"Tomorrow? I could use one now." Her teeth were chattering by the time she got Olivia buckled in and seated herself in the front. And while she was thankful for heated seats, she could hardly wait to don some fleece pajama bottoms, her fuzzy robe and her slippers.

She eyed her sleeping daughter in the back seat, then shifted her attention to Hawkins as he turned into her drive. "Did you have fun tonight?" She wasn't sure if, maybe, he just didn't like surprises or what, but he'd seemed a little off after their arrival. Not near as excited as he'd seemed when they'd left her house, and she wished she knew why. Perhaps he was simply overwhelmed.

"Yeah. It was nice to have some time with Gabe and Jake. More than we get in Sunday school."

"You went to school with them, right?"

He nodded. "They were a few grades behind me. But in Hope Crossing, everyone knows every—" He slowed the vehicle.

"What is it?"

He gaped at whatever lay beyond the windshield. "This doesn't look good."

"What?" She followed his line of vision, panic welling when she spotted the debris strewn across the drive. Tree limbs, wooden planks and crumpled metal. "My house!"

"Easy." He settled a warm hand against her chilled arm. "Your porch light is still on, so I think your house is fine."

She eyed him across the console. "What are you worried about, then?" Because the lines etched in his brow hadn't been there before.

He put the vehicle into Reverse, backed up and slowly turned until the SUV's high beams illuminated the barn.

Leaning forward, she visually followed the lights and tried to focus. A split second later, she felt her eyes widen while her brain finally grasped what she was seeing.

How? She attempted to speak, but no words came out. Instead, only short bursts of air moved past her lips. Mouth agape, she stared at her beautiful old barn. One corner was completely gone, and the rest of that end had collapsed as though the supports had been kicked out from under it.

She shook her head, hoping to make the scene go away, all the while blinking back the tears that threatened.

Feeling a hand on her shoulder, she turned and buried her face into Hawkins' shoulder as one by one the ramifications rained down on her like shrapnel. What about all the stuff that was inside? The tree stands, the saws, measuring sticks and countless other items that were vital if she was going to open the Christmas tree farm. Were they still there, or had they been blown across the countryside?

And what about her trees? Were they still there or had they been swept away, too?

A sob escaped her lips.

Hawkins' hold tightened. "I'm here." His breath was warm on her ear as he smoothed a hand over her hair. "You and Olivia are safe. That's all that matters."

While that was true, so much more hung in the balance. She'd moved here for the sole purpose of opening the tree farm. To prove to her parents that her ideas were more than silly notions. That she was capable of building the kind of life *she* wanted, one her daughter could be proud of.

When her whimpers subsided who knows how long later, he set her away from him and brushed the hair away from her face. "There's nothing we can do about the barn tonight. But I need to make sure your house is secure before I leave."

Amid the glow of the dashboard, she stared into his eyes, wondering what she would've done if he hadn't been with her. If she'd come home alone to face what could be the destruction of her dream.

She nodded her agreement.

"I need to clear a path first, though." He maneuvered the vehicle so the headlights again illuminated her driveway, then exited to clear the debris, tossing it on either side of the drive. "It wasn't as bad as I thought," he said when he returned. "What was in front of us was the bulk of it. The rest of the way appears clear."

Shivering, she kept her gaze riveted to the drive as he continued to the house and parked a few feet from his truck.

"Oh, no!" She straightened. "Your truck."

He cast a glance through his window. "Looks fine from here."

Under the porch lights, both on the front of the house and outside the kitchen, everything appeared the way she had left it, save for all the leaves and twigs that hadn't been there before.

"You and Olivia stay put while I inspect the outside of the house. Make sure there are no broken windows or anything."

"How will be you be able to see?"

"I've got a high-powered flashlight in my truck." He reached for the door. "I shouldn't be long."

After locating said flashlight, he sent her a thumbs-up before disappearing around the back of the house.

She hugged herself, suddenly missing his embrace. Once again, Hawkins had been there to rescue her. And while she wasn't exactly thrilled that she'd repeatedly needed his help, she was grateful he was in her life. Hawkins *was* a hero. Yet, like most heroes, he bore the scars of battle, even if they weren't visible.

His poor heart had been brutalized by that woman in Alaska. He deserved so much better. If only Annalise could let go of her insecurities. Because like a bee to nectar, she was drawn to him. But she had her own issues. Issues that had just been greatly amplified. At this rate, she was beginning to wonder if she'd even be able to stay in Hope Crossing. She was counting on the income from the Christmas tree farm to pay her property taxes. But with no barn, not to mention whatever other problems were hidden in the darkness, how could she open?

Finally, the beam of his flashlight appeared as he moved to the front of her house. And a few minutes later, he rejoined her.

He eased into the driver's seat long enough to turn off the engine. "Everything looks good. Why don't you go unlock the door, and I'll bring Olivia in?"

She did as he suggested. The night air was downright cold now, and the accompanying breeze only made it worse. She'd definitely be turning on the heater tonight. How she prayed it worked.

Olivia barely stirred when Hawkins laid her in her crib minutes later. Annalise kissed her daughter's chubby cheek and tucked a blanket around her before joining Hawkins in the kitchen.

"What's that noise?"

He pointed to the stove. "I added some water to your kettle and put it on to boil in case you wanted something hot to warm you up."

The way he anticipated her needs warmed her more than any hot drink ever could. "Care to join me? I've got some cocoa mix. Besides, it's the least I can do before sending you back out into that cold."

He grinned. "I spent a long time in Alaska." He tugged one hand from the pocket of his jeans long enough to poke a thumb toward the door. "It's practically balmy out there."

Disappointment had her looking away. She was kind of hoping he'd stay.

"But yeah, I'll have a cup. I don't want to keep you up, though. There'll be a lot to do tomorrow, so you'll need as much rest as possible."

She almost laughed out loud. Based on what she'd seen out there tonight, she'd be surprised if she slept at all. With so much uncertainty hanging over her head, she'd never be able to shut her mind down.

"And it might not be a bad idea to go ahead and call your insurance company," he continued. "I'm sure they'll have adjusters headed this way before sunrise, so you may as well get your name on the list. The sooner they get here, the sooner you'll be able to determine your next move."

How she wished he'd used another word. Depending on what transpired in the coming days, a *move* might be her only option. Because without the Christmas tree farm, she didn't know if she could afford to stay.

Chapter Eleven

Hawkins sat in the pew of Hope Crossing Bible Church Sunday morning, wedged between his mother and his sister, finding it difficult to focus on the pastor's message. Instead, his thoughts were centered on a noticeably absent Annalise. He prayed she was merely sleeping late. That despite the angst that, no doubt, had her tossing and turning for who knows how long, she'd finally given in to the rest her body and mind needed.

Bible in hand, one finger tucked between the pages of First John, he suspected that wasn't the case, though. Especially since Olivia had crashed on the way home and had, likely, awakened much earlier than Annalise would've liked.

Now as Pastor Woodson offered up a closing prayer and they stood to sing, Hawkins knew he had to check on Annalise. Because no matter how uncertain he was about her feelings toward him, he knew how he felt about her. Strong enough that he couldn't leave her to muddle through the chaos and uncertainty facing her right now. She was a strong woman. Stronger than she believed herself to be, thanks to those who'd failed to recognize her true value. And he wasn't about to let her give up on herself or the tree farm. He'd fight for her dream even if she didn't have the strength.

After letting his family know he was leaving and why, he sought out Gabriel and filled him in on what had happened, asking their class to pray.

"You got it," Gabe said. "And if there's anything we can do—food, grunt work, whatever—just let me know."

"I will." Hawkins shook his friend's hand. "Thanks, man."

The air was crisp and the sun shone brightly as he moved across the parking lot to his pickup. Once inside, he prayed all the way to Annalise's that she would feel more hopeful today. That the sassy woman who'd worked alongside him that day they started shearing the trees would make a reappearance, as opposed to the devastated Annalise who'd cried on his shoulder last night.

When he pulled into her drive seventeen minutes after leaving the church, he paused to study the barn through the windshield. Amazing how half of the structure was able to stand erect while the other half had virtually caved in on itself. The remaining portions of the rusted metal roof appeared curled in one way or another as though the wind had tried to peel them off. Meanwhile, many of the dark weathered planks lay scattered about.

He let go a sigh. There was no way the barn could be saved. And he could only pray that Annalise had had the forethought to add replacement coverage to her insurance. Otherwise…

No, he wasn't ready to think about that. He was more interested in the status of the trees.

After parking, he exited his truck as the kitchen door opened. Annalise stood on the other side of the storm door, wrapped in a fluffy robe.

"Brr." She shivered as he stepped inside. "It's freezing out there."

"Nah." He closed the door behind him. "Only forty-five, according to the thermometer in my truck."

"Need I remind you we were in the eighties yesterday?"

Olivia toddled toward him and latched on to his leg.

He stooped to pick her up, his gaze trained on her mother. Her eyes were puffy and red, and yesterday's sparkle was gone. "I didn't see you at church. Did you sleep late?"

She finger-combed her tangled hair. "No. I couldn't muster the energy to go." Pointing to the window over the sink, she added, "Just for the record, things don't look any better in the light of day than they did last night."

While she was right in terms of the barn, she seemed to be overlooking the most important part of the Christmas tree farm.

"We'll see about that." He stood Olivia on the floor again. "Why don't you two get dressed, and we'll take a ride to check on the trees."

"That sounds cold, to say the least."

"Just what we need to get into the Christmas spirit. Dress warm, and we'll bring a couple of blankets."

"Spoken like someone who's used to Alaska weather."

He pointed toward the bedrooms. "Sweaters. Long johns. Heavy coats. Now! Whatever you need to keep warm."

Taking hold of her daughter's hand, Annalise glared at him over her shoulder, her brows drawn together. "Since when did you become a drill sergeant?"

"Go!"

"By the way," Annalise said as they climbed into the utility vehicle a short time later, "the insurance adjuster called this morning to say he'll be out before noon tomorrow." She covered a yawn.

"Did he wake you up?"

"No." Holding her daughter in her lap, she draped a soft throw over the both of them. "Olivia had that honor."

"Sorry." He fired up the engine, deciding he'd try to entertain the little one later and allow Annalise to take a nap.

The cool air made its presence known the instant they pulled out of the garage. Both Annalise and Olivia's cheeks were tinged pink in no time, not to mention the tips of their noses.

"All right, let's see what we're dealing with." He started at the section that was home to some of the largest trees. "So far, so good," he said as they continued on to the next section.

Annalise didn't say a word, but even with her sunglasses on, he could tell she was scrutinizing every tree. And by the grace of God, not a one of them appeared to have suffered any damage. Something that should've put a smile on her face. Yet as they neared the house a little over an hour later, her frown only deepened. Even as his mother's Tahoe rolled up the drive with Gloriana in the passenger seat.

Leaving the UTV parked at the side of the house, Hawkins took hold of a blanket-wrapped Olivia as Annalise moved her sunglasses to the top of her head. Side by side, they made their way down the drive to meet them, eyes glued to the gravel, mindful of any debris.

"Oh, honey." Mom tore her gaze away from the barn as she neared Annalise and wrapped her in her arms. "I'm so thankful you and Olivia are all right." She set her away and palmed her cheek. "Thank God you decided to stay at Glory's until the storm passed."

Gloriana hugged her next. "I know you're heartbroken about the barn." Releasing her, she added, "But look at the bright side. Now you can build something to suit *your* needs."

Annalise shook her head. "There's not enough time. We're supposed to open in less than three weeks."

"We'll find a way to make do." Gloriana took Olivia from him.

"Besides," he said, "the trees are what folks will be coming for, and they're fine."

"We can use the shed and the garage," said his mother.

"What about the tractor and the other equipment?" Annalise seemed to grow more overwhelmed as she looked around. "Where will we store them?"

"The tractor will fit in the garage," he said. "And since we'll be using the red truck as part of the decor, there'll be plenty of space for it."

"But the barn was supposed to be the centerpiece. It was the anchor for everything and added ambience. Without it, there's nothing special." Tears shimmered in Annalise's blue eyes. "You'll have to excuse me." With determined steps she turned and started toward the house.

Watching her retreating back, Hawkins said, "Y'all keep an eye on Olivia for me, please." He hurried after her. As he neared the corner of the house, he hollered. "Annalise? Stop."

To his surprise, she did. Hands stuffed in the pockets of her coat, she refused to turn around.

Moving in front her, he settled his hands on her shoulders and dipped his head to meet her gaze. "You once told me that you wanted a fresh start for you and Olivia. And then, out of the blue, you inherited this place. Even though you intended to sell it, you fell in love with it instead. You said you felt as though God had heard your prayers and had given you the desires of your heart."

She looked everywhere but at him, swiping at the tears that streamed down her cheeks.

"Surely you don't believe that was the end of it. That God is going to up and leave you now?" He lowered his hands. "That storm was no surprise to Him, and neither is this damage." Hawkins swept an arm toward the barn. "Yeah, it stinks. Yeah, we've got a lot of work ahead of us. But I am confident that God knows exactly what we need. And one way or another, He will meet those needs." He reached for her hand. "We're all here for you. Me, my family. Please tell me you're with us. That you're not giving up on God or this extraordinary place we've all come to love."

She stared at their entwined fingers. Sniffed a few times. But she didn't say a word.

Suddenly, a horn honked.

They turned as a handful of vehicles poured into her drive.

Annalise sniffed, swiping a hand across each cheek. "Who is that?"

Recognizing Gabriel's truck, he smiled. "The cavalry." Hawkins again took hold of her hand. "Come on."

Mom was pointing out places for folks to park as Hawkins and Annalise approached Gabe's truck.

He rolled the window down. "Heard you could use a little help out here."

"A little?" A stunned Annalise took in all of the other vehicles.

Gabriel exited his pickup. "We've brought lunch, trash bags, gloves, tools and folks to do the grunt work. Just tell us where to start."

"Well," said Hawkins, "the barn is on hold until the

adjuster comes tomorrow. But I think there's enough cleanup needed to keep everyone busy."

"And when you're ready to tackle the barn—" Gabe looked from Annalise to Hawkins and back "—just let us know. You're one of us now, Annalise. And we take care of our own."

As the group that also included Tori and Jake began unloading their vehicles, Annalise pulled Hawkins off to the side, tears again shimmering in her eyes, except this time there was a smile on her lips.

"Did you know about this?"

He shook his head. "I let Gabe know I wouldn't be in class and told him what had happened here, but that was it."

She glanced toward the people bustling around. "Looks like God's done it again." Her focus shifted back to Hawkins. "All my life I've never found that place where I felt like I truly belonged. Until now."

He couldn't help smiling. "I told you He wasn't done." And Hawkins prayed the Big Guy had even more in store for the both of them.

Under a beautiful, sunny sky, enveloped by a glorious seventy degrees, Annalise looked out over her property, feeling almost overwhelmed by the transformation her little farm had undergone in the last ten days. Though, she supposed, the same could be said about her. She'd gone from complete despair when her barn was destroyed to feeling more hopeful than ever. All thanks to Hawkins Prescott. Instead of coddling her, he'd challenged her to take the focus off herself and trust that God was still with her and was still in control.

Now as she looked around the place she was blessed to call home, all she could say was "Wow." God had moved in a mighty way, orchestrating things she never would've imagined. Things far beyond her Sunday school class coming out to help with cleanup.

As soon as the insurance adjuster had departed the next day after deeming her barn unusable, she and the Prescotts began emptying the old structure. Thankfully, the items they'd moved from the shed were on the side that was spared so they were easily retrieved.

A track hoe and dozer came in later to remove portions of the collapsed roof until they were able to get the tractor out. Then, after salvaging as much of the old barnwood as possible, the rest of the barn was demolished and the pad cleared. All before the end of that week.

While they were emptying the barn earlier in the week, a builder from their church who specialized in pole barns had come by, saying he'd heard about the tree farm and how his family had been looking forward to its opening. Then he offered to provide the materials for a new barn at cost. So as soon as Annalise settled on a design, the wheels were set into motion.

The Saturday following the storm, dozens of people from church and around town descended on her property and built her new red barn with a white roof and trim, even cupolas, in a day and a half. Yet while she'd have to wait until the season was over to add concrete floors, it was a sacrifice she could live with. She was just thrilled to have a barn again.

Not just any barn, though. One with character, designed to meet her specific needs. Again, thanks to Hawkins, who'd helped her focus on her vision and what she wanted. So while the new barn had the same footprint as the original, the layout was completely different, starting with covered porches on each of the longer sides. The one at the back was strictly for utilitarian purposes, such as storing the tractor and other implements. Meanwhile, the front porch had been adorned with the weathered wood from the old barn—Hawkins' idea—to create an inviting facade that would welcome guests in search of that perfect Christmas tree or visiting the small store she'd added behind a set of double doors.

Best of all, guests would see it as they approached instead of having to be guided around to the far end of the structure, as with the old barn. Now, sliding doors on the ends of the new barn allowed easy access to a larger area she'd decided to use for shaking the trees, as well as baling them for transport.

Now, with their grand opening only ten days away, and volunteer and employee training slated for this Saturday, she stepped onto the barn's front porch late Tuesday afternoon to survey the acres of Christmas trees that stretched farther than she could see. How strange it would be to have some—hopefully many—of them gone. Though, they'd soon be replaced by new saplings, and the process would begin again. A process Tom would, thankfully, guide them through.

Her phone jangled in her pocket.

She pulled it out, a thrill jetting through her when she saw Hawkins' name on the screen. To his dismay, he'd had to drive into Houston today for a meeting. Perhaps he was letting her know he was on his way back. She'd told him she was putting a roast in the Crock-Pot, anticipating he'd want to join her and Olivia for supper.

"Hello."

"How's my favorite Christmas-tree farmer?" His words made her smile.

"Blessed. Thrilled. Overwhelmed."

"Just letting you know I'm going to be late getting back. But I still plan to tackle that floor tonight."

The idea of a dirt floor in the store was a little more than she could wrap her mind around, so after some research, she'd decided to cover it with some interlocking rubber tiles to at least create the illusion of a floor. And then had jumped on Hawkins' offer to assist her with the installation.

"That's all right. The roast is in the slow cooker so it'll be ready whenever. And as for the tiles, I may not be an engineer like you, but I'm pretty sure I can manage them. Unlike a jigsaw puzzle, it's simply squares, and they all fit together no matter which way you turn them."

"I know, but I'd at least like to help you."

She stepped from the porch into the sun, savoring its warmth. "I guess your meeting ran late, huh?"

"No, my truck broke down east of Brenham. Tow truck's coming to get it."

She straightened, eyeing her watch. It was 3:36. "Do you need me to come and pick you up?"

"Already called my sister. She's on her way."

Disappointment had Annalise's shoulders sagging. Why hadn't Hawkins asked her to pick him up? With all he'd done for her since she arrived in Hope Crossing, she certainly owed him. She could've gone just as easily as Gloriana. Especially with Olivia at day care.

"You should've called me."

"Annalise, we both know you have enough on your plate right now."

And he didn't? Yet that had never stopped him. He'd spent more time at her place than his own since the storm.

"Tow truck's here. I'll see you when I get back."

The line went dead. Annalise stood there, staring at the phone, nostrils flared, her heart pounding. Suddenly, she wasn't so sure she wanted to see him.

Despite everything they'd been through, his insistence

that he believed in her, when push came to shove he'd dismissed her, calling on his sister instead of her. And that cut her to the quick.

Fuming, she eyed the pallet of black rubber tiles sitting just outside the doors of the store. She could stand a little manual labor.

Pushing up her sleeves, she tore open one box while studying the instructions on another. Confident in her assumption that it was no more difficult than a children's puzzle, she set to work inside the store. She was halfway through when she heard a horn honking outside.

Straightening—something not too easy when she'd been stooped over for the past hour—she glimpsed an unrecognizable truck outside the door. Why would they be honking?

She slipped outside the door as the driver stopped in front of the barn.

"You Annalise Grant?" he asked as he exited the vehicle.

"I am."

"I have a special delivery for you." He moved to the bed of his truck.

Special delivery? "I didn't order anything." At least not in the last two days.

"No, ma'am," he said as he approached. "But someone else did." He leaned the rather large parcel—at least two feet by three feet—wrapped in craft paper against the wall. "And I'm supposed to tell you that you're not allowed to open it until you receive further instructions."

Further— "From who?"

With a brief tug on the brim of his cap, he returned to his truck. "Have a good evening."

After he pulled out of the drive, she contemplated opening it. But it was time to pick up Olivia. And when she returned, Gloriana's Jeep Cherokee sat in her drive. With Hawkins leaning against it.

The sky was growing dark as she parked in her usual spot. Hawkins approached. And while he started for Olivia's door, Annalise quickly rounded the vehicle to cut him off. Her daughter had already formed an attachment with him. No point in intensifying it when Annalise was about to give him what for.

"Look, I know you're probably upset with me for not asking you to pick me up."

With her daughter on her hip, she slammed the car door. "Guess you had time to think about that on the drive with your sister, huh?" She started toward the house.

"Actually, I thought about it before I called her."

Her steps slowed. She turned to look at him. The lines etched into his brow told her that he knew she'd be upset he'd asked Gloriana to pick him up instead of her. Yet he'd done it anyway.

"But you still called her."

He dragged a hand through his thick hair. Only then did she realize he wasn't wearing his usual attire. The ball cap was gone. And he wore a maroon button-down over his dark-wash jeans. Of course, he'd met with his boss.

"Only because I needed you here." His dark eyes bore into hers, lines of frustration pleating his brow.

"That doesn't make sense. Why would you *need* me here?"

Hands on his hips, he turned away, his frustration evident. "Was there a delivery today?"

She'd almost forgotten. "Yes. Why? Is it something for you?"

Pinching the bridge of his nose, he released a sigh. "Where is it?"

"Porch on the barn."

He looked at her now. "Will you please accompany me over there?"

Why did her knees have to go weak at the pleading in his eyes?

He promptly intercepted Olivia, smiling. "Come on."

The package was right where she'd left it, beside the door. "It's yours for the taking," she said.

"It's for you," he said.

When her gaze jerked to his, she found him staring at her. A hint of uncertainty in his eyes.

"I'd planned to be here when it came, but things didn't play out the way I'd intended." He gestured toward it. "Please. Open it."

She took hold of the package and set it atop the stack of tiles that remained. Then she ran a finger beneath the tape, allowing the craft paper to fall open.

Her heart stuttered. Why was Hawkins being so serious? What was in here?

Reaching inside, she lifted the thin piece of wood. As she turned it around, tears sprang to her eyes, even though she didn't want them to. She was supposed to be reading Hawkins the riot act. But how could she when she now understood why he'd wanted her here?

"It's the logo you and Gloriana designed." His voice was rough behind her.

She stared at the sign with the rustic white wood-look background, a red Christmas truck in the center with a pine tree sticking out the back and the words *Hope Crossing Christmas Tree Farm* at the top in the same green font she and Gloriana had decided on.

"I thought it might look good hanging here on the porch."

Of course it would.

Before she could think better of it, she set the sign down, turned and hugged his neck. "It's beautiful."

"I was hoping you'd like it."

Though she longed to linger, savoring the scent of fresh air, earth and Hawkins, she forced herself to step back. "It's perfect." Her gaze drifted to the spot near the door. "And I know just where I want to hang it."

"Right here?" He pointed.

She laughed. "Exactly."

Chapter Twelve

With a plan under his Hope Crossing Christmas Tree Farm ball cap and a prayer on his lips, Hawkins maneuvered his truck—replete with a brand-new fuel pump—up Annalise's drive the following Tuesday afternoon.

Thanksgiving was only two days away, and the grand opening of the tree farm the day after that, so today he was determined to steal Annalise away from all of those little details that had been consuming her every waking hour lately and see to it she had a little time for herself.

She'd been so busy since the barn collapse, so laser-focused on the opening and making sure people would have the best experience possible as they searched for their perfect tree, that by the time she realized she'd forgotten her own, the best trees would be gone. And he wasn't about to let that happen. No, he wanted Annalise to have the cream of the crop. Whatever she deemed the perfect tree.

Now if only he could figure out how he was going to pry her away from all of those minute details consuming her time and attention.

He eased to a stop alongside the barn's front porch, noting the classic red pickup that now sat at an angle midway between the red shed and the trees. And its doors bore magnetic versions of the sign he'd given Annalise last week.

He couldn't help but smile. "Nice."

Exiting his truck, he moved to the porch. Despite the dirt floor—which Annalise swept routinely, just as she would any other floor—she, his mom and his sister had created an inviting space that would beckon even the most finicky shoppers. The posts were wrapped with garlands that were a mix of pine and cypress boughs, while two small trees adorned with white lights sat in large, galvanized buckets on either side of the green double doors that each bore a wreath. A couple of white rocking chairs sat beneath a window to the right of the entrance, separated by an old barrel turned checkers table, while the left side prominently displayed the sign he'd given Annalise, right in between the door and the walk-up checkout window for those who preferred not to go inside the store.

Lowering his gaze, he noted a new addition beneath the sign. He chuckled at ol' Frosty, who stood there with his cane looped over his arm while he smiled at Hawkins. Seemed the old relic wasn't about to let a simple barn collapse do him in either.

After wiping his feet on the mat, Hawkins entered the store where holiday music filled the space.

Annalise glanced up from one of several displays she'd been meticulously working on all week and smiled. "You're just in time. My little helper here keeps getting under my feet."

"That's because she wants your attention."

"Always." She turned from the display and picked up her daughter. "But I'm not complaining." She kissed Olivia's chubby cheek.

A pleasant aroma had him inhaling deeper. "It smells like Christmas in here."

"Doesn't it smell great?" When Olivia voiced her displeasure over being held, Annalise again stood her on the makeshift floor.

And when she promptly headed in Hawkins' direction, he could only smile.

"Janette Carey pours her own candles," Annalise continued. "She has some of the most incredible fragrances." She pointed to a small display in the corner as he picked up Olivia. "Oh, and check out Bonnie Bachman's ornaments." She pointed toward the far wall. "They're gorgeous. All hand-painted."

He accepted one of Olivia's juicy, openmouthed kisses. "Thank you, munchkin. I guess your mama picked you up early today, huh?"

"Yes. I finished my report last night and sent it off, so I decided to go ahead and get her so we could spend the rest of the week together." Moving beside him, she again kissed Olivia's cheek, and suddenly, all he could think about was how nice it must be to be on the receiving end of one of Annalise's kisses.

"Congratulations."

"Thank you." She practically beamed as she clasped her hands together. "And I have more news."

"Your parents are coming for the grand opening?"

"No." Though her countenance briefly fell, she quickly recovered. "But then, I didn't expect them to."

"Annalise, they're your parents. It's okay to expect them to want to see their daughter's dream come to life."

"I know." She shrugged. "But that's not how my parents roll."

"So what's your news?"

"I talked with Becky over at Plowman's. They're not

only bringing some quick breads and cookies to sell this weekend, they're creating some cookie-decorating kits, too." When he lifted a brow, she continued. "The boxes will have an assortment of baked cutout cookies along with colored icing and sprinkles so folks can decorate cookies right along with their tree."

"I have a feeling those'll be a hit."

"I think so, too." Glancing around the space, she seemed to catch her breath. "I cannot believe how my little Christmas tree farm is turning into an all-out seasonal event."

She was right about that. In addition to what was going on in the store, the church youth group was going to be selling hot chocolate and spiced cider to raise funds for summer camp while the volunteer fire department would be cooking up barbecue both Friday and Saturday.

"And you were worried."

She looked suddenly shy. "I'm a work in progress."

"Aren't we all." He winked. "So what else do you have to do right now?"

She looked around. "Nothing, really. Though, I could arrange and rearrange forever."

"No way." Still holding Olivia, he reached for Annalise's hand. "I'd like you to indulge me."

"How?"

Rubbing his thumb over her soft skin, he said, "I want *you* to pick out *your* Christmas tree. I'll help you cut it down, bring it in, get it set up. Then—" he shrugged "—maybe we can decorate it."

Her nose wrinkled in that cute way she had. "I was just going to put up my old prelit one. Eventually."

His brow shot up as he released her. "That's a bit hypocritical, don't you think? You want people to buy your fresh trees while *yours* comes from a box in the attic."

"When I was little, I used to beg my parents for a real tree."

"And?"

"They always said real trees were too messy, too labor-intensive, and they were never perfect the way an artificial tree was."

"Last time I checked, Christmas wasn't about perfection. I mean, Jesus was born in a stable. That's about the most *imperfect* scenario I can think of."

She cocked her head. "And yet He lived a perfect life."

"He did." He nudged her with his elbow. "So…what do you say we make your childhood dream come true and find you the most perfectly imperfect tree on your property?"

The pink in her cheeks coupled with the sparkle in her eyes did strange things to his heart. Things that were as delightful as they were frightening.

"Why don't you take Olivia and the two of you grab some jackets while I hook the flatbed to the tractor, and I'll meet you at the house."

Several minutes later, he pulled up to her house, noticing a stark contrast between it and the barn. Turning off the tractor, he climbed down as Annalise and Olivia emerged from the kitchen door.

"Where're you going?" Annalise followed him to the front of the house, Olivia in her arms.

He pointed to the front porch that was void of any holiday decor. "This is wrong on so many levels."

"What do you mean?"

"Look at that." He pointed toward the barn. Then, taking hold of her shoulders he turned her to face the house. "Now look at this. What's wrong with this picture?"

She bit her bottom lip. "I guess I've been spending so much time and energy on the barn that I kind of forgot about decorating the house."

Arms crossed over his chest in an I-told-you-so manner, he nodded. "We're going to rectify that tonight. Y'all hop on the trailer while I drive."

Falling in beside him, she grinned. "Start in section two, row fifteen." She glanced up at him now. "There are a couple of pines I've had my eye on."

He smiled. "You got it."

She made her decision within minutes, then he started the cut before allowing her to take over and fell the tree.

"That was strangely satisfying," she said, still holding the saw.

"Uh-oh. Guess we'll have to start calling you Paula Bunyan."

She simply waved him off. "Whatever."

They took the tree to the barn and set it in the shaker for several seconds to eliminate any loose needles, then she grabbed a stand while he loaded the tree back on the trailer.

Once they returned to the house, they spent a few minutes moving furniture so the tree could go in front of the window. Then, while she ladled up the chili she'd had in her Crock-Pot, he positioned the stand and filled it with water before making a fresh cut on the seven-foot pine and placing it in the stand.

"That smells so good." She stood in the opening between the kitchen and living room a short time later, chili bowl in hand.

Beside her with his own bowl, he glanced her way. "I assume you're talking about the tree, but how can you smell it over the chili?"

She touched a finger to her nose. "I have a good sniffer." She heaved out a breath. "I just realized something, though."

"What's that?"

"I don't have any lights." She looked at him. "Like I said, I've always had a prelit."

"What do you mean you don't have any lights?" He pointed outside. "Every time I turn around you're adding more lights to something somewhere on the farm. You and Gloriana must have an entire truckload of those things. Don't tell me you used them all."

"Oops." She blushed. "I forgot about all the ones I have stashed in the barn. I guess I could use them in here, huh?"

He could only shake his head. "What a novel idea."

She popped him in the arm. "Be nice."

"I'm always nice."

"Yeah, you kinda are."

Looking down at her, he wondered if he'd ever been happier than in this moment. God had given Annalise the desires of her heart in the form of a Christmas tree farm. Suddenly Hawkins couldn't help wondering if God was granting his in Annalise. Then again, he'd been wrong once before. If he was wrong this time, he wasn't sure he'd be able to bounce back.

After their Thanksgiving feast at Francie's, Annalise and the Prescotts had caravanned back to the Christmas tree farm to make more fresh wreaths and garlands and do a final once-over to make sure everything was ready to go when they opened the gate Friday morning. And while Annalise had collapsed into bed just before eleven, she felt like an eight-year-old on Christmas Eve, anticipation keeping her awake half the night.

Now as she bounded into the kitchen to turn on the coffee maker well before sunrise, an unmistakable sound had her entire being cringing.

No. It couldn't be.

While the coffee brewed, she moved to the door, jerked it open and turned on the light. A pained sigh spilled from her mouth as her body sagged. Her worst nightmare was playing out right before her eyes. Rain. On their opening day.

Closing the door, she shuffled back to the coffee maker as it spit out its final effort, grabbed a cup from the overhead cabinet and filled it before sagging against the counter. No one would want to search for the perfect tree in a cold rain. Why would they, when they could simply go to one of the big-box stores where they could choose between a perfect prelit, a blue spruce or some other variation of pine that'd been shipped in from someplace that had snow?

She blew across the steaming liquid before taking a sip. Then cringed when she realized she'd forgotten to add creamer.

Reaching into the refrigerator for the peppermint mocha, she heard her phone buzz on the counter. She closed the door then looked at the screen while she poured. A text from Hawkins.

Happy opening day! Are you up and ready to go?

After returning the creamer to the fridge and taking a hearty sip, she replied.

It's raining. She accentuated her statement by adding a frowny-faced emoji.

The little reply bubble danced on her screen.

It's only a drizzle.

Whatever. It's still wet stuff falling from the sky. Who's going to want to come out in that?

Another bubble.

No Debbie Downers today. Get dressed, I'm on my way.

She huffed out a sigh. "Fine."

Returning to her bedroom, she grabbed a quick shower then swiped some BB cream on her face along with a couple strokes of mascara before donning skinny jeans and a white, long-sleeved compression shirt she then topped with one of the green *Hope Crossing Christmas Tree Farm* T-shirts she'd ordered for employees and volunteers. After pulling on her duck boots, she gathered her hair into a ponytail and topped it with a tree-farm ball cap.

Eager for a second cup, she grabbed her mug and started back toward the kitchen until Olivia's jabbering had her doing an about-face. She'd just finished changing her daughter's diaper and getting her dressed when she heard a knock on the door.

"Sounds like Mr. Hawkins is here." She put her daughter down on the floor, and the child promptly headed for the kitchen.

"Awks. Awks." Olivia's recently expanded version of Hawkins' name had the corners of Annalise's mouth tilting upward.

Annalise opened the door, and Hawkins stepped inside, all smiles.

"Good news." He rubbed his hands together. "The rain stopped, and there are breaks in the clouds."

"Really?" Annalise whisked past him as he picked up Olivia to see the sky brightening.

"I checked the forecast," he added. "And they're calling for clearing skies and sunshine the rest of the day."

Thank You, God. And forgive me not only for complaining but for doubting You.

As she started to close the door, she noticed a white van coming up the drive. "That must be Plowman's with the baked goods."

"You go meet them. I'll take care of Olivia. Has she had breakfast?"

"No." Grabbing her keys from the hook on the wall, she rattled off some quick instructions before heading out the door. Hurrying across the yard, she was pleased to see only the occasional, tiny puddle.

Before she made it to the store, Gloriana's Cherokee rolled up the drive.

"You're just in time," Annalise called out when Hawkins' sister emerged.

It took the two of them, along with Brenda from Plowman's, a good hour to get the boxes of baked goods unloaded and either displayed or stored so they could replenish as needed. By then, employees, volunteers and the rest of Hawkins' family had arrived. And as the sun shone brightly in the eastern sky, Annalise wondered what she would do without them. Gloriana was like the sister she never had. Francie the sort of mom Annalise aspired to be. And Hawkins?

He was one part big brother and one part best friend. Which left one more part: uncertainty. Hawkins was the kind of man women dreamed of. Kind, patient, encouraging, not to mention incredibly handsome. But could he be her Prince Charming?

Thankfully, she didn't have any time to contemplate. Vehicles were lined up on the road before nine, and they had a steady stream of customers throughout the gloriously beautiful day.

By the time things wound to a close, Annalise was

exhausted. But in a good way. Smoke still wafted from the firemen's barbecue pit as she gathered everyone in front of the store for an update.

"I cannot thank you all enough for opening your hearts to me. I'm new to Hope Crossing, but you all have embraced me, my daughter and our business, and that makes you pretty special in my book." She had to pause to clear the sudden lump in her throat. "Just so you'll know, we had a stellar day. The youth group sold two hundred and fifty cups of hot cocoa and a hundred and thirty cups of spiced cider."

Everyone applauded. "The fire department sold over two hundred pounds of barbecue."

The applause was punctuated by the firemen whooping.

"And over five hundred Christmas trees will be bringing holiday cheer to people in and around our community." The celebration was so loud she had to shout over them. "And that's just day one!"

When things grew quiet, she continued. "Again, thank you from the bottom of my heart for helping make this day a success. Now let's get some rest so we can do it all over again tomorrow."

A short time later, as the sun set and everything was locked up, she and Hawkins started toward the house with Olivia.

As they walked, he nudged Annalise with his elbow. "Can I interest you in a frozen pizza?"

"Wow, big spender."

"Considering it'll be coming from your freezer." He lifted a shoulder.

She reached for the screen door. "You're not fooling me, mister."

"I'll be happy to put it in and take it out of the oven,

though. Ask me nicely and I might even cut it." He pushed open the door and waited for her to pass.

"You really know how to impress a girl, don't you?" She stepped inside.

He followed, closing the door behind them. "Well, you did it. You had a dream, and you made it come true."

She removed Olivia's jacket and watched as she headed straight for the living room and her toys. "I had a lot of help. Starting with you." She looked up at him, feeling more gratitude than she could express. "You saw past my failings and believed in me anyway. Even when I didn't believe in myself. No one has ever done that before."

He watched her intently. "Then, that's their loss." He took a step closer. "Annalise, the more I've gotten to know you, the more I appreciate how genuine you are. Sure, you have your weaknesses, but we all do. I think it's Ecclesiastes that says, 'Two are better than one…for if they fall, one will lift up his fellow.'"

Disappointment had her looking away. She was just one of the guys.

Reaching out, he cupped her cheek and coaxed her to look at him. "Before you go thinking I see you as just a friend, let me assure you, that is not the case at all."

Between the warmth of his hand and the smoldering look in his eyes, she could barely breathe.

"I am drawn to you like—" He chuckled. "There are a bunch of clichés zipping through my brain right now, so let's just say that I see you as a lot more than just a friend. And I think—hope—you see me in a similar light." Removing his hand from her cheek, he held it up. "But if you don't, please be gentle with me. Or simply rip off the Band-Aid and—"

Fisting his shirt in her hands, she pushed up on her toes and kissed him. Rather adamantly, at that. Maybe not the wisest move, but since she couldn't get a word in edgewise, she had to find some way to put his fears to rest.

Obviously stunned, he simply stared down at her, his hands cradling her elbows as she broke the connection.

Half smiling, she said, "I get your point."

He cleared his throat. "In that case, let me prove it again, without so many words." Lowering his head, he touched his lips to hers, softly, allowing her to experience their warmth and tenderness mixed with a hint of passion. Enough to let her know exactly how he felt about her, should she have any doubt. Which she did not. She now knew what that third part was. And it was coupled with an unfamiliar trust that encouraged her not to over-think it.

Chapter Thirteen

From where Hawkins sat atop the tractor late Sunday afternoon, the Christmas tree farm was enjoying as much success today as it had the previous two. And they hadn't even opened until one.

Between Friday and Saturday, Annalise had sold just under nine hundred trees. At that rate, they'd be out of trees long before the planned closing date of December 18. Even without the youth group's hot-drink sales and the fire department's barbecue, the place was still crawling with people today. He supposed the seventy-degree temps could have something to do with it. Not what most folks would consider Christmas weather but still a great day to be outside.

He maneuvered the tractor and trailer around the perimeter of each section, looking for folks waiting with their perfect tree so he could return them to the front for checkout. The only speed bump this entire weekend had been yesterday's arrival of Paul and MaryAnn Adams. And only in part because it squashed his hopes of another kiss anytime soon. His heart still went into a full gallop when he recalled the way Annalise had let him know he was doing too much talking.

But that wasn't what had him bugged about her parents' visit. Actually, he was pleased they'd had a change of heart and come to see this fantastic holiday escape their daughter had created. He just wished they were more supportive and less condescending. Just because they'd never be interested in living in the country or cutting down their own Christmas tree didn't mean Annalise's choices were wrong.

Yeah, it'd been a struggle to hold his tongue a couple of times yesterday. It wasn't that he was trying to find fault with Paul and MaryAnn; on the contrary, he was looking for ways to connect with them. But when they looked down their noses, he was always at the end of them. So he'd politely declined Annalise's invitation to join them for dinner last night. Something he now regretted, fearing he'd fed her to the wolves. So when she'd asked him to stay tonight, he couldn't say no.

Since her parents were business owners, his hope was to help them recognize that Annalise was a smart businesswoman in her own right. One who'd quickly become an important part of the Hope Crossing community. Who knew? Perhaps he'd even be able to find some common ground with her parents. When he did, he'd latch on to it because they were her parents, after all. And if he hoped for any kind of a future with their daughter…

Where had that come from?

Your heart, doofus. Stop trying to deny you're in love with Annalise.

The only thing worse than having a conscience was having a vocal one. And his was right on point. Annalise was everything he never knew he wanted in a woman. She was real and tenderhearted. Spunky. He was comfortable with her while still being struck by her beauty. A beauty that came from within, not applied every morning. She fit in seamlessly with his family, too. And stirred feelings he never expected after what had happened with Bridget. Except this was different. Deeper.

Looking back, he realized that what he and Bridget had had was purely superficial. Oh, he'd wanted it to be more, but that's kind of hard when the other person isn't sincere.

Spotting a family of four and another of five just ahead, he brought the tractor to a stop midway between them, hopped off, double-checked that they'd tagged their trees, then hoisted the pines onto the back of the trailer while the families situated themselves at the front end. Then he headed back to the store as the sun crept toward the western horizon and only a handful of guest vehicles remained on the property.

A short time later, the tractor was parked under the overhang at the back of the barn, and Annalise was bidding employees and volunteers goodbye until Friday.

Only a few dregs of light remained when he came alongside her. "So how many trees for the whole weekend?"

She practically beamed. "If my count is correct, eleven hundred and nine."

He gave her a high five. "That's amazing." Shaking his head, he added, "And to think I was skeptical."

"Maybe, but you've certainly put in your fair share of work to help make things a success."

"It was my pleasure." Just like every moment he spent with her. "Everything locked up?"

"Yes."

"I assume your parents are in the house."

"With Olivia, yes." She chuckled. "They're probably ready to be rescued. This afternoon may be the longest stretch of time they've ever spent with her."

While Annalise behaved as if that was completely normal, he found it rather sad. Especially since they'd lived so close to her parents prior to moving here. Did the Adamses have any idea what they were missing out on by not being a part of their granddaughter's life? They needed to check their priorities.

Annalise pushed open the door a short time later, and they were greeted with aromas that had his mouth watering already.

"Are you cooking another roast?"

She perched a fist on her hip and glared at him. "Yes. I put it in the Crock-Pot this morning so I wouldn't have to worry about cooking tonight."

Removing his boots, he glanced her way. "Why so defensive? I mean, A, I'm a beef guy. And B, I've had your pot roast. It's delicious."

Her hand dropped as pink suffused her cheeks. "Good." She cut a glance into the living room before moving to the counter and peering through the glass lid. If he had to guess, it would be that someone had made a comment about either the roast or her method of cooking it long before he got here.

"Awks!"

He turned to see Olivia toddling toward him, her ever-present smile in place. "Hey there, munchkin." He lifted her and tossed her in the air.

Her giggle had to be one of the sweetest sounds on God's green earth.

He tucked her into the crook of his arm. "Have you been having fun with your grandparents?" Still holding her, he moved into the living room where Paul sat on the floor. He'd been playing with Olivia. Meanwhile, MaryAnn was perched on the edge of the recliner, her feet crossed at the ankles.

"She seems to enjoy playing ball." Paul held up the colorful orb.

Seems to?

"What do y'all think about the Christmas tree?" He gestured to the pine adorned with more white lights than he'd have thought a tree could hold.

"Smells great." Still holding the ball, Paul bent his knees and rested his arms on them. "I noticed it as soon as we walked in yesterday."

"It's very…festive." MaryAnn eyed the tree as though it had some contagious disease.

"Dinner will be ready shortly." Annalise stood between the living room and the kitchen. "The roast needs to rest while the rolls are in the oven."

When her mother didn't offer to help, Hawkins stood Olivia beside her grandfather. "Do you need any help?" Yes, he was eager to escape. "I can set the table."

Annalise sent him an appreciative smile. "Thank you."

Not about to make Annalise look bad, he fixed each place setting just the way his mother had taught him when he was little, adding a placemat and napkin, and making sure each piece of flatware was in its correct position.

When they finally settled around the table, Annalise's father said grace before they began filling their plates.

Hawkins accepted the platter from Paul and added a good helping of meat and potatoes to his plate, along with a couple of carrots for color. "I have to commend you both." He eyed each of Annalise's parents. "Your daughter is quite the trooper. Not only did she jump right into all that growing Christmas trees entailed, she didn't let something as challenging as losing her barn defeat her."

Annalise cut a carrot into tiny pieces for Olivia. "I'd like to amend that statement. I was ready to admit defeat, but you wouldn't let me."

"That's because I knew, deep down, that you're not a quitter. And so did a lot of other people." He cut his meat. "I don't know if Annalise told you, but the entire Hope Crossing community rallied around her to make sure her tree farm opened on time." He rested his utensils on his plate, pulled out his phone and began scrolling through photos. "They cleared away the old barn and built her a new one in record time." He passed the phone to Paul. "Scroll through there." He watched as the man's expression morphed from disinterested to impressed.

Paul passed it to his wife. "Take a look at what they did, MaryAnn."

She slowly skimmed through each of them. "I do like red for the barn. And the wood on the front is a lovely touch."

Hearing MaryAnn compliment something Annalise had done made Hawkins want to cheer.

Then she added, "It must have cost a pretty penny to get things done so quickly."

"Not at all." Annalise wiped her mouth with her napkin. "The builder provided the materials at cost, which insurance more than covered. And everyone who helped clear and build did so simply because they wanted to help. Nobody expected anything in return." She cast a smile Hawkins' way. "Although, I did make sure they were well-fed."

MaryAnn handed Hawkins his phone. "That's what they say now, but mark my word, somewhere down the road they're going to expect something in return."

Hawkins couldn't hold his tongue. "Pardon me, ma'am, but no, they won't. Folks around here aren't like that. At least the majority of them. We take care of each other."

"The world could use a lot more of that," said Paul.

Olivia chose that moment to grow fussy.

Hawkins hoped he hadn't caused it. That she hadn't sensed his displeasure with her grandmother.

"She didn't have a nap today." Annalise pushed her chair out. "I'm going to go ahead and give her a bath. You all can keep eating." After lifting Olivia from her high chair, Annalise sent him an "I'm sorry" look before disappearing down the hall.

She needn't be concerned, though. He could hold his own. And he'd be nice. He'd just continue to sing her praises, praying her parents would realize how special she was.

"Hawkins," Annalise hollered from her bedroom a short time later.

"Whatcha need?"

"Can you get me a towel from on top of the dryer, please?"

Eyeing her parents, he said, "Excuse me."

He grabbed the towel and made his way down the first hallway, then made a left into the next one before turning right into the en suite in Annalise's room. For some reason she preferred bathing Olivia in there. Perhaps because it wasn't quite as tight as the bathroom in the hall.

"Here you go."

"Thanks."

Olivia splashed, getting him wet. Then she giggled.

"Hey, you got my socks wet." He leaned over the tub and splashed her back. A very tiny, baby-size splash, anyway.

She startled and blinked as a few droplets landed on her face. Then she giggled again.

He set a hand on Annalise's shoulder. "I'd better get back out there before your parents get the notion there's something inappropriate going on in here."

He hadn't made it to the second hallway that led to

the kitchen when he overheard something that stopped him in his tracks.

"If she's unable to pay her taxes, this could be the leverage we need to convince her she's in over her head and she should come back to Dallas."

He felt his eyes widen. There was no way he'd let that happen.

But was what they were saying true? Annalise couldn't pay her taxes?

While the tree farm had had a profitable weekend and, Lord willing, the following weekends would be just as lucrative, Annalise had also put out a lot of money for incidentals, food and decorations.

His chest tightened. He couldn't risk it. Though he had yet to tell her, he loved Annalise. And her kiss had told him everything he needed to know about her feelings for him.

He couldn't allow her parents to manipulate her again. He'd see to it Annalise remained in Hope Crossing to follow her dreams. Not only because she was important to him, but because he'd seen how much joy the tree farm had brought her despite all the obstacles. And if this weekend was any indication, the Hope Crossing Christmas Tree Farm was fast on its way to becoming a tradition not only for Annalise but for people all around Hope Crossing.

Annalise was relieved when her parents left that Monday morning after opening weekend. Since then, she'd been up to her ears in a project for work, allowing little more than dinner and a couple of short hours with Hawkins. She missed the long days they used to spend together before they both went back to work.

The tree farm's second weekend had been every bit as

robust as the first. It did her heart good to see hundreds of people enjoying themselves, some driving two-and-a-half hours from San Antonio. Seemed they'd heard one of Gloriana's radio interviews.

Now as Annalise returned from picking up Olivia from day care Tuesday, she pulled alongside her new black mailbox adorned with a big red bow. They were only a week into December and Annalise was already counting down the days until Christmas.

She eyed Olivia in the back seat. While her daughter might be too young to experience the anticipation of this season, Annalise was growing antsier by the day. Between Hawkins and his family, this Christmas was bound to be unlike any she'd ever experienced.

She retrieved her mail, thoughts of Hawkins sending a quiver up her spine. No one had ever made her feel the way he did. As if she mattered and her opinion was important. He challenged her to believe in herself.

Thoughts of seeing him tonight had a contented sigh escaping her lips as she closed the mailbox. No one had ever had as much faith in her as Hawkins. And that had rendered her helpless to keep her feelings in the friend zone. Even if she was afraid to acknowledge how deep they truly went.

She pulled into her drive, admiring the festive atmosphere of her little farm. From the pine-garland-draped front porch of her house to the garage and shed adorned with icicle lights to the new barn that was dressed to the nines, the place made her smile. And she could hardly wait to do even more next year when she wouldn't be so pressed for time. That was assuming all of her buildings remained intact.

After parking, she grabbed the mail, tucking it into the diaper bag as she gathered Olivia. The late-afternoon air was cool, but not cold. Though a gentle breeze tossed Olivia's downy hair.

"Let's go start dinner, shall we?" Even if it was only frozen enchiladas. "Mr. Hawkins will be here soon." She held her daughter's hand as they moved up the steps to the kitchen door.

"Awks." Olivia smiled.

Just then, the lights on the garland around the door turned on.

The child's eyes went wide. "Ohh…"

Ah, yes. The wonder of Christmas through a child's eyes.

Inside, she settled Olivia in her high chair with a snack before turning on the oven to preheat. After grabbing a handful of grapes for herself, she sat down beside her daughter and sorted through the mail.

An envelope bearing the name of the county tax office captured her attention. Perhaps it was a reminder to pay. Something she planned to do once the tree farm closed for the season.

She ran a finger under the sealed flap and pulled out the paper inside. Unfolding it, she scanned the page, her gaze narrowing. It was a receipt confirming her taxes had been paid.

A burning sensation sparked in her belly and quickly burst into flames. Once again, her parents had overstepped. While she'd adamantly told them, in no uncertain terms, that not only was she not selling the tree farm but she was capable of paying her taxes, they'd completely ignored her.

Grabbing her phone, she dialed her mother, but it went straight to voice mail. So she tried her father, only to meet with the same results.

She let out a frustrated groan and grabbed the enchiladas from the freezer. When would her parents finally accept that she's a grown woman able to take care of herself?

Maybe the same day she saw a pig soar past her window.

As she ripped open the box, there was a knock at the door. She glanced out of the window to see Hawkins' truck.

He was smiling when she jerked the door open, though his mood quickly evaporated. "Uh-oh." He stepped inside. Closing the door behind him, he added, "What's wrong?"

"My parents."

"What did they do this time?"

"They paid my taxes. *After* I specifically told them I could do it myself. I know what they're doing. They're trying to talk me into moving back to Dallas, and they think by paying my taxes they can hold that over my head as if I owe them something." She grabbed the pan of enchiladas. "Well, that is not going to fly. I'm putting a check in the mail to them tomorrow. I refuse to be indebted to my parents. If they choose not to cash the check, that's on them, but I am not going to let them manipulate me."

Opening the oven, she all but threw the pan inside. When she turned around, Hawkins was right there, a sort of hesitant, lopsided smile on his lips.

"If you'll calm down for just one second, I have something I need to tell you."

She willed herself to draw in a deep breath, then slowly exhaled. "Okay."

He placed his hands on her shoulders. "It wasn't your parents who paid your taxes. It was me."

Her gaze searched his. "What? No."

"That night I had dinner with you and your parents, you had me bring you a towel for Olivia. When I was on my way back to the kitchen, I heard them say that you couldn't afford to pay your taxes."

"And you believed them?"

"Not at first. But then I heard them say they were going to use your inability to pay as leverage and convince you to return to Dallas."

Shaking her head, she stepped away from the intensity of his dark eyes.

"I don't remember what they said after that. All I knew was that I didn't want them to have that kind of power over you. And I couldn't bear the thought of you leaving. So I went to the courthouse the next morning and paid your taxes." He shoved a hand through his thick hair. "So if you still want to write that check, just make it out to me."

Annalise felt as though she'd been punched in the gut. All of his pep talks and words of encouragement, they'd been nothing but lies. He didn't believe her any more capable than her parents or Dylan ever had.

Fists balled at her sides, she glared at him. "You're just like them."

His confused gaze turned her way.

"You don't think I'm capable of taking care of myself either." The calm in her voice belied the inferno raging inside of her. "And you certainly didn't trust me enough to come and talk to me about what you overheard."

"Annalise, please."

She ignored him and kept going. "Instead you automatically assumed I needed someone to step in and rescue me." She shook her head, disappointment morphing her anger into grief as reality smacked her in the face. "You're no different than anyone else in my life."

Olivia began to whimper.

Moving to the door, Annalise pulled it open. "It's time for you to go. I don't need your help anymore. I'll send you a check for the taxes, as well as your portion of revenue from the tree farm."

"Annalise?" The pain in his eyes as he moved toward her had her looking away.

"Goodbye, Hawkins."

After what seemed like an eternity, he finally slipped through the door. She closed it behind him, twisted the lock, then went to console her daughter while her heart crumbled into a million pieces.

Chapter Fourteen

Under a canopy of oak trees, Hawkins set another piece of wood atop the chopping block in his front yard the next afternoon. Moments later, he swung his ax with the full force of his frustration, splitting the log in half. He'd been at it for over an hour, hoping to ease some of the tension between his shoulders, but his muscles were still knotted. He'd hurt Annalise in the worst possible way, and now he was paying the price.

She didn't want him in her life.

What bugged him most of all was that she was right. He should have talked to her first. But he hadn't done that. Instead, he'd reacted, allowing his fear to get the best of him. Fear of losing her. Yet he'd lost her anyway.

He placed another log on the block as tires rolled down the gravel path toward the cabin. Looking up, he saw Gloriana's SUV.

Great. He wasn't in the mood for conversation.

While his sister parked, he took aim, hitting the log and sending the two pieces flying in opposite directions.

"That's a lot of wood," she said when she approached. "You expecting another norther?"

Dragging his forearm over his sweaty brow, he simply watched her.

Dressed in a plaid flannel shirt and jeans, her ponytailed hair covered with a camo ball cap, she stopped opposite him and slid her fingers into her pockets. "So what's the story with you and Annalise?" She placed one booted foot atop a log. "I was at the tree farm earlier. Annalise said she fired you. When I asked why, she said I should talk to you, so here I am."

Fired? He puffed out a laugh. Was that all he'd been to her? An employee?

Instead of responding, he reached for another piece of wood. Split it, then reached for another.

Before he could set it on the block, his sister snatched it from his hand. She always had been a scrappy one.

"Talk to me, Hawk. I'm not blind. I've spent the last two months watching you and Annalise fall in love. Now you both have long faces and bloodshot eyes, and *you're* no longer helping out at the tree farm. What gives?"

He eyed the live oak leaves rustling overhead. "What makes you think we were falling in love?"

She cast him an I'm-not-stupid look. "Oh, I don't know. Maybe it was the fact that you were always together. Or that glimmer in your eyes whenever she was around. The way you encouraged her, giving her the confidence to keep going when she was ready to give up."

While he couldn't refute any of her observations… "None of those things have to do with falling in love."

"Maybe not by themselves, but all rolled together?" She took a couple of steps toward him, her gaze fixed on his. "You each made the other a better version of themselves."

He just stared back at her. This wasn't their first battle

of wills. "Spoken like someone who's still in the honeymoon phase of her marriage."

"Or one who's suddenly super-sensitive thanks to the new life growing inside of her."

"Whoa, what?" Breaking eye contact, he slammed the ax into the chopping block and moved beside her. "Are you serious? You're pregnant?"

Looking up at him, she nodded, happy tears brimming in her eyes. "Found out this morning, so needless to say, Justin and I haven't told anyone yet."

"Not even Mom or Kyleigh?"

"No." She held up a scolding finger. "So don't you *dare* say a word."

He whooped, lifting her off the ground in a hug. Until he thought better of it and carefully set her back down. "Sorry. I guess I probably shouldn't have done that." He didn't want his brother-in-law coming after him for jeopardizing his wife and unborn child.

"Don't be silly." She waved a hand. "You're fine. It's not like I'm going to break. Though, I won't be riding a horse for a while. I'm kinda bummed about that, but it won't be the last sacrifice I'll have to make for this child."

Hands on his hips, he stared down at her. "Man, you and Justin didn't waste any time. You've been married less than three months."

Her gaze narrowed. "Okay, first of all, at thirty-five my biological clock is ticking. Second, we might want to have more." She shrugged.

"So when are you planning to let everyone else know?"

"That's to be determined. However, you and I both know that once Mom finds out, the rest of the world will know in short order."

He looped an arm around her neck and kissed her

forehead. "Congratulations, sissy. I'm honored to be the first to know."

"So…" She peered up at him. "Why don't you return the favor by telling me everything that happened between you and Annalise."

Leaving his arm where it was, he turned and started toward the cabin with her in tow. "I should've known there was a catch." But he also knew that she cared. "How about a cup of coffee?"

"Got any decaf? Pregnant women aren't supposed to have caffeine."

He managed to find a couple of decaf pods, and soon they were sitting in two of the four spindled barrel chairs around his kitchen table while he explained what had happened with Annalise's parents and how, in desperation, he'd taken matters into his own hands.

"I didn't want her to lose her dream. Not when she'd worked so hard." He stared into his cup. "But she was right. I behaved like everyone else in her life. I assumed she couldn't make the payment, so I stepped in and made it for her, purely for selfish reasons."

"Because you were afraid she'd leave."

He nodded.

Gloriana reached for his hand. "That's not selfish, Bubba. That's love."

He lifted a shoulder.

"Don't go shrugging me off. You *do* love her."

He wrapped his fingers around his mug. "And what makes you so certain about that?"

"Because you paid her taxes."

Sometimes his sister baffled him. "So?"

"After what happened with Bridget? Do you have any idea how huge a move like that is?"

Okay, so maybe she was right. Not only had he paid

Annalise's taxes, he'd never hesitated or questioned himself over it. He just did it.

Staring into his now-empty cup, he said, "I would never do anything to hurt Annalise or Olivia. Nor do I want to see them hurt or manipulated by anyone else."

"Which is why you paid her taxes?"

He pushed away from the table. "And look where that got me." He'd gone from contemplating a life with her to being cut out of it altogether. And there was nothing he could do to change that.

Annalise stood behind the counter made of old barn wood, counting tree tags in the store shortly before closing the following Saturday. And if her numbers were correct, they had less than thirty trees left in this year's inventory.

She glanced out the walk-up window to see the number of today's guests dwindling. If she was right, they'd be closing for the season tomorrow instead of next weekend.

"There you are." Gloriana stepped through the front door.

"Perfect timing." Annalise motioned for her. "I need you to double-check my numbers against these tags."

"Sure." Gloriana joined her behind the counter.

Annalise watched while she counted, thankful that Gloriana hadn't pressed her about the falling-out with her brother. Not only that, she'd done whatever she could, shy of driving the tractor, to make sure nothing had fallen through the cracks in his absence. An absence Annalise felt with every fiber of her being.

Yet while she missed Hawkins, she wasn't willing to risk losing control of her life again. It had taken her more than thirty years to take a stand and make choices based on what she wanted, not what was dictated to her. She wasn't about to turn back now. Not even for the man she loved.

"My calculations are the same as yours," Gloriana said with a smile.

"Then, it looks like tomorrow will be our final day of the season."

"Why?"

"Our inventory is almost gone."

The corners of Gloriana's mouth slowly lifted. "I knew this place was going to be a hit."

They squealed and hugged like a couple of teenagers.

And Annalise felt just as giddy. "I can hardly wait to get started on next year. I have so many ideas."

"Me, too," said Gloriana.

"Not that you'll be around all that much." She eyed her friend's tummy. Gloriana had shared the baby news with her yesterday.

"Says the lady with a toddler, who put in more work than anybody this year. At least mine won't be walking."

"I'm so happy for you." Annalise gave her another hug.

Peering up at her, Gloriana said, "If only you weren't so miserable. But I don't blame you for being upset with Hawkins. Like you said, he could have at least talked to you about things first."

The last thing Annalise wanted to do was talk about Hawkins.

"You know—" Gloriana pressed her lips together when the door opened and a woman with auburn hair walked in, saving Annalise.

"Someone mentioned you all have some cookie-decorating kits," said the woman, who looked to be in her midthirties.

Annalise scurried from behind the counter. "We sure do. How many would you like?"

The woman's brow knit. "Hmm. How many cookies in each box?"

"A dozen."

She smiled. "In that case, I'll take three of them."

Annalise grabbed a stack from the shelf.

"I love whatever fragrance that is you've got going on in here," the woman added. "Is that a candle?"

"Yes, ma'am. I believe that one is called Holly and Spice and Everything Nice. They're made locally."

"Would you happen to have five of them? They'll make great gifts. And I like to support small businesses."

Gloriana crossed to the candle display to investigate. "I guess it was meant to be, because we have exactly five left."

"Oh, good." The woman gave a satisfied handclap as she made her way to the counter. "I live in Dallas but came down to visit my grandmother for the weekend. She lives in the assisted-living facility, but said she'd heard so much about this place that I should stop by, and I'm glad I did." She looked at Gloriana. "The cookies are for Grandmama and her friends to decorate."

"Aww," said Gloriana. "That's a great idea."

"I moved here from Dallas a few months ago." Annalise wrapped the candle jars in tissue paper before adding them to the craft-paper bag. "What part of town do you live in?"

"Not too far from the Galleria. How on earth did you end up in Hope Crossing?"

Annalise chuckled. "I inherited a Christmas tree farm."

"You're kidding! That has to be the coolest story I've ever heard."

"Thank you. It's a very different lifestyle, that's for sure."

"Do you love it, though?"

Even more so when she'd had Hawkins to share it with. "Yeah, I do." She added the last candle to the bag. "I'm Annalise, by the way."

"Jillian."

After accepting payment and handing Jillian her purchases, Annalise said, "Your receipt is in the bag, and I wrote my email address on it just in case you ever contemplate moving to Hope Crossing."

"Thank you. I don't foresee that happening. However, I might need some cookies and candles next year at this time." Jillian pushed the door open. "Merry Christmas!"

"Merry Christmas!" Annalise and Gloriana replied in unison.

"Well, that was a nice interlude." One Annalise hoped brought an end to any talk about Hawkins.

She checked her watch. "It's past closing time. I need to get outside so I can talk to everyone before they leave." She grabbed her quilted barn coat. "I need to let them know that tomorrow will be our last day."

A beautiful sunset blazed just above the horizon as she exited the store. Her employees were clustered near the old red truck, beanies on their heads, hands burrowed in the pockets of their coats.

"You all look like you're ready to get home where it's warm," she said as she approached. "Thank you for making this another great day. Because of you, we are almost out of tree inventory for this year."

"Whoa," said one fellow.

"For real?" a girl asked.

Annalise nodded as she glimpsed Kyleigh coming out of the house with Olivia. "However, just because we're being forced to close early doesn't mean you'll be out any money. You will still be paid for next week."

Every pair of eyes went wide.

"I do expect to see you all here tomorrow, though, so y'all get on out of here and go find someplace warm."

A few of the girls hugged her as they left, while a couple of boys fist-bumped her.

As they continued to their vehicles, Kyleigh neared with a grinning Olivia. She looked so cute bundled in her puffy purple coat and pink knit hat.

"That is *too* cute."

Annalise turned to see Gloriana approach.

"I blew out the candles and shut down everything inside," she said.

"Thank you." Annalise faced her daughter again. "There's my girl." She scooped the child into her arms. "Did you have fun with Kyleigh?"

"Awks."

How could one syllable wreak so much havoc on Annalise's heart? Olivia had grown attached to him. As he had her, Annalise would venture to guess.

Gloriana looked at Kyleigh. "Have you got all your stuff?"

"It's still in the house."

"We need to head out, so why don't you go grab it."

"'Kay." With that, Kyleigh took off toward the house.

And Gloriana turned her attention to Annalise. "I just have one thing to say, and then I'll shut up."

With a lead-in like that, Annalise was ready to bolt herself. But she stayed put.

"While I don't blame you for being upset with my brother, I'm quite surprised he did what he did. I mean, after what he went through in Alaska."

Annalise recalled the tortured look in his eyes when he'd told her how Bridget had conned him out of all that money and humiliated him.

Yet, he paid your taxes.

Gloriana shrugged. "He thought he was doing a good deed for a friend." Her gaze bore into Annalise. "Though, dare I say, you are far more than just a friend."

"I'm ready, Mom," Kyleigh hollered across the lawn.

"Be right there." Gloriana smiled. "I'll see you tomorrow, my friend." She gave Annalise and Olivia a hug before joining her daughter.

After making sure things were locked up, Annalise headed to the house.

Inside, Annalise removed Olivia's hat and helped her out of her coat before shrugging her own off.

"I think we'll keep dinner simple tonight. How about a grilled cheese sandwich?"

"Ees." Olivia looked up at her with those innocent blue eyes. "Awks."

Annalise smoothed her daughter's flyaway hair. "Not tonight, baby." More like never. Even if she was ready to forgive him, he might not be willing to do the same.

While Olivia played with her toys, Annalise set to work on their supper. She set the cast-iron skillet on the stove, turned on the flame, then added butter to the pan. All the while, Gloriana's comment kept rolling through her mind.

I'm quite surprised he did what he did. I mean, after what he went through in Alaska.

Annalise thought back to the day he'd told her about Bridget. She remembered his pained expression as he revealed what had happened. And her own disgust over the woman's actions.

Placing the bread slices in the pan, she thought about the way Hawkins constantly encouraged her, bolstering her confidence. How he bragged on her to her parents. No one had ever believed in her the way Hawkins had.

She set the cheese atop the bread, then used a spatula to flip one side on top of the other. Hawkins wasn't afraid to give his input, but he also listened to her. Helped her without diminishing her. If it hadn't been for him, there would've been no tree farm this year. But he'd refused to let her give up her dream.

A lump formed in her throat as she removed the sandwiches from the skillet and set them on a plate. While her parents and Dylan had routinely acted out of a desire to control her, Hawkins had acted out of love.

I couldn't bear the thought of you leaving.

Through unshed tears, she looked around her kitchen, the very place where she'd torn into him, accusing him of being just like her parents. Yet, it was also where he'd given her one amazing, toe-curling kiss that had left no doubt as to how he felt about her.

Cutting her daughter's sandwich into bite-size pieces, she said, "Come eat, Olivia."

Once she was in her high chair, Annalise sat beside her with her own plate and blessed their food. "Eat up, baby girl. Because we're going out. Your mama's got a wrong she's going to do her best to make right."

Chapter Fifteen

Sweat beaded Hawkins' brow as he turned into Annalise's darkened drive and continued toward her house. What was wrong with him? This was nothing more than a social visit.

Gloriana had called with the news that Annalise had sold almost all of her trees, so he wanted to congratulate her by way of bringing her some of his mother's divinity. Because despite blowing his opportunity to win Annalise's heart, he hoped they could still be friends. He was proud of her and wanted to let her know. No matter how much his heart ached.

Besides, he was tired of moping around the cabin. When college-football playoffs no longer interested him, it was time to take a break. And even if Annalise didn't welcome him with open arms—he wished—just seeing Olivia's smile was sure to do wonders for his aching heart.

The light was on in the kitchen when he parked beside Annalise's SUV and turned off the engine.

Leaning against the headrest, he sucked in a breath. *Lord, please, if You could at least make this a pleasant, not awkward, visit, I'd greatly appreciate it.*

He grabbed the festive tin beside him and stepped out into the chilly night air. Talk about a silent night. Not even a—

Just then a cow bellowed across the road.

Never mind.

He'd barely set his foot on the bottom step when the door opened.

Annalise stood there, Olivia on her hip, looking more than a little surprised. "Hawkins?"

Keep it together, Hawk.

"I came by to congratulate you. I hear you're about out of trees."

"Less than thirty. I was shocked."

"That's great." He held up the tin. "I thought you could celebrate with some of my mom's divinity."

Her shoulders seemed to relax. "I *love* divinity." She pushed the screen door open. "Come on in."

"Awks!" Olivia clapped her chubby little hands before holding them out to him. Her way of asking him to hold her.

"I'll trade you." He passed the tin to Annalise while reaching for Olivia with his other arm. "Hey there, munchkin." He instinctively kissed her cheek, savoring the smell of baby shampoo. How he'd missed this little one and her adorable antics. But that wasn't what had him tossing and turning these past few nights.

His gaze shifted to Annalise as she opened the container and took out a piece of candy. Just seeing her had him feeling like he could breathe again.

She took a bite, her eyes closing.

"Pretty good, huh?"

Looking at him again, she said, "This may possibly be the best divinity I've ever had."

"Good, I'm glad you like it. I'll be sure to let Mom know."

Olivia wiggled, so he stood her on the floor.

Straightening, he captured her mother's gaze. "I'm proud of you, Annalise. Your dream has become a reality."

"Come on, Hawkins. We both know I didn't do this alone. I had a *lot* of help. Starting with you."

He tamped down the hope he felt rising.

"You were with me throughout this entire journey. Even when you didn't want to be. You never gave up on me, nor would you let me give up on myself."

"Because I believed in you and your dream."

She glanced into the other room where Olivia played with her toys. "There's something I'd like to ask you."

His hope-ometer climbed once again. "Sure."

"The last time we were together, you said you couldn't bear the thought of me leaving." She tilted her head. "Why was that?"

Because he loved her. Couldn't imagine life without her. Had entertained thoughts of forever.

But what came out was "Because you'd worked so hard."

"So did you. You were right there with me every step of the way. Encouraging me. Believing in me, even when I didn't believe in myself."

When he hesitated, she took a step closer. "We've been through a lot together these last couple of months. From the moment I arrived in Hope Crossing, you've been there. Even when you didn't want to be. I was wrong to send you away, Hawkins, because a life without you isn't really living at all. You gave me the courage not only to fulfill my dreams but to open my heart again. So I'm asking you again." She caressed his cheek. "Why did you want me to stay?"

The warmth of her touch was just what he needed. "Because I love you." He took her hand from his cheek and held it against his chest. "That Sunday after the storm, the pastor preached about love and how there is no fear in love. Annalise, I know you've been hurt, that there are gaping wounds in your heart, but if you would give me the opportunity, I would like not only to heal them but prove to you that love—real love—is so much more than either of us has experienced before."

The tears that had pooled in her beautiful blue eyes spilled onto her cheeks. "You've already shown me more love than I deserve. I'm sorry I hurt you, Hawkins. Can you forgive me?"

"Sweetheart, there's nothing to forgive." Wrapping his arms around her, he lowered his head and kissed her with all he had, making sure she'd never again question his feelings for her. But before he could truly seal this deal, there was one more thing he had to do.

Hawkins brought his truck to a stop in front of the stately Dallas home a little more than a week later. He'd contacted Annalise's parents through their real-estate office, letting them know he was in town on business and asking if he could speak with them. And he'd be lying if he said he hadn't been more than a little pleased when they said yes.

Wearing a navy blazer over a white button-down with dark-wash jeans, he stepped from the truck and started up the walk. The sound of his boots moving across the flagstone pavers that carved a path across the landscaped yard echoed the thudding of his heart.

Lord, forgive me if I'm going about this the wrong

way, but I want the Adamses to see their daughter in a different light. To see just how smart she is. And this is the only way I can think of to get through to them.

He stepped under the portico of the French-style two-story stone home, noting the strings of large white bulbs outlining the structure. Turning, he glimpsed the miniature lights wrapped around shrubs and the oak tree in the middle of the small yard. Though he was certain they'd been put there by professionals, he was pleased to see Annalise's parents weren't Scrooges.

He rang the bell and moments later Paul appeared on the other side of the substantial iron-and-glass double doors.

"Hawkins," he said as he swung open one of the doors. "Welcome." Moving aside, he motioned for Hawkins to enter the massive foyer adorned with a lavishly decorated twelve-foot Christmas tree.

"Thank you for seeing me."

Closing the door, Paul said, "I have to confess, we were rather surprised when you called."

"I'm sure you were. But I have something I'd like to share with you and MaryAnn that I thought would be best done in person."

Cocking his head ever so slightly, Paul studied him. "Does my daughter know you're here?"

Hawkins drew in a breath and released it. "She knows I'm in Dallas. I did not tell her I was planning a visit with you and MaryAnn, though."

Paul sent him a knowing wink. "Sometimes we have to keep a secret." He motioned toward the back of the house. "Come join us in the study."

Hawkins followed Annalise's father down a long hallway with the same hand-scraped wood floors that stretched throughout the first level until they reached a room with oak paneling, bookcases and coffered ceilings.

MaryAnn rose from one of four pale blue upholstered chairs as they entered and started toward them. "Hawkins, it's good to see you again." She extended her hand.

He took hold, noting that she seemed different. More relaxed. "You, too, ma'am."

"Can I interest you in some coffee?" She motioned to the carafe and holiday-themed cups sitting on a tray atop a side table.

"No, thank you. I've had my quota for the day." To his surprise, she actually chuckled. Nothing condescending about it, just a genuine chuckle.

"Please—" Paul motioned to one of the chairs "—have a seat and tell us what it is you'd like to discuss." He sat down, glancing at his wife. "Although, I think we might have some idea."

Preferring to stand, Hawkins cleared his throat, glad he wasn't wearing a tie, because he'd certainly be loosening it right about now. "Actually, I'd like to show you something." Reaching into his breast pocket, he pulled out the sheet he'd printed before leaving Hope Crossing.

He handed it to MaryAnn, who had yet to sit. "I know Annalise spoke with you last week, excitedly sharing the news that she'd had to close the tree farm earlier than expected due to a higher-than-expected volume of sales, but I thought you all might like to see just what that equated to."

MaryAnn had donned her reading glasses and was studying the page, her brow pinched. "Gross receipts," she mumbled.

While her husband moved beside her, Hawkins watched

as she scanned the page, her eyes widening as they neared the bottom. "This is six figures."

"Yes, ma'am. A few times over," Hawkins couldn't help adding.

She looked at him now. "All of this is for Christmas trees?"

"Ninety percent of it. Though, there were also things like fresh wreaths and garlands, the store sales."

"That's *very* impressive," said Paul.

"Yes, it is. And it was all because of your daughter. Annalise may not be interested in real estate, but she's got a mind for business. Couple that with a passion for making others smile and, well, I'd say God truly blessed her efforts."

Still holding the paper, MaryAnn pressed a hand to her chest as she eased into her own chair. "I-I had no idea." She appeared to grow a little misty.

"Annalise may have different interests than the two of you, but that doesn't mean she's not competent."

Removing her glasses, MaryAnn looked up at him. "I believe you've been trying to tell us that since that first time we visited our daughter in Hope Crossing."

Hawkins felt his cheeks heating. "Yes, ma'am. And I apologize if I came on a little too strong."

"It's because you care about her," said Paul.

"Yes, sir. Very much. Which brings me to the other reason for my visit today."

Chapter Sixteen

This was the kind of Christmas Annalise had always dreamed of.

Surrounded by the sights, sounds and smells of Christmas, she grabbed another thumbprint cookie from the abundance of goodies spread across Gloriana's kitchen island Christmas morning, savoring the laughter and conversations that filled the house.

Behind her, Kyleigh helped her mother transfer oven-fresh muffins to a basket, all the while doing her best to convince Gloriana they should open presents right now.

In the adjoining family room, Justin stoked the fire in the stone hearth while Hawkins sat on the floor atop a large neutral-toned geometric rug, trying to distract Olivia from the plethora of brightly colored gifts beneath the beautifully decorated Virginia pine. He seemed relieved when Bill's daughter, Alli, who'd come in from Austin for the holidays, joined them, providing a nice distraction for Olivia.

Meanwhile, the tweed and leather sofa situated in front of the windows that overlooked the backyard held the biggest surprise of all. Annalise's parents were not only conversing with Francie and Bill, they actually seemed to be enjoying themselves.

Of course, this wasn't the first time they'd surprised her since arriving two days ago. Her jaw had definitely dropped when they came rolling up her driveway in an RV. Of course, not just any RV. No. This one was a great big motor coach complete with a king bed, bath-and-a-half, flat-screen TV and plenty of space. They said it was a combo traveling office and home away from home. Translation, they could come and visit her and still live somewhat in the fashion to which they'd become accustomed.

Whatever the case, it seemed to make them happy. They'd been much more relaxed this time than their last two visits. They'd even told her how proud they were of her, not only for the success of the tree farm but for sticking to her guns and following her dream. And that was the best Christmas present she could've received.

She turned toward Gloriana, who was stirring something on the stove. "You're sure there's nothing I can help you with?" Hawkins' sister had waved off her previous offer. "In your condition, you could probably use a break. You know, put your feet up."

"I'm fine."

Hawkins came alongside Annalise. "Hey, I just realized I left one of my gifts at the cabin. Care to ride down there with me?"

She hated to leave Gloriana with all this work. Then there was her daughter. "What about Olivia?" She peered around him to see Alli playing with her.

"I can watch her," said Kyleigh.

On the opposite side of the island, Gloriana said, "We'll all watch her."

Hawkins smiled, reaching for Annalise's hand. "Come on. We won't be gone long."

Reluctantly, she let him drag her outside. The weather was warm enough that no coats or jackets were needed.

She eyed him as they climbed into the cab of his truck. "Do you really expect me to believe that you couldn't make this little jaunt all by yourself? I mean, you said yourself that it wouldn't take long."

"Yeah, but I enjoy your company."

"Uh-huh." She eyed him across the console as they wound past the Prescott Farms barns. "Say what you like, but I know what you're up to."

"You do?" His voice went flat.

"You know, if you wanted to steal a kiss, we could've just snuck outside on the porch." Like they'd done at her place when her parents were there.

He grinned as they neared the cabin. "I really do need to grab a gift. Though, I will never turn down one of your kisses."

"Who says I'm offering?"

"I like it when you get spunky."

She shook her head as he came to a stop.

They climbed out and continued toward the cabin.

Reaching for the doorknob, he leaned toward her. "I love you."

Hearing those three words on his lips never failed to melt her heart. "I love you, too." Then she pushed up on her toes to meet him halfway for a kiss. "There," she said. "Are you happy now?"

"Very." He opened the door, and they stepped inside. "It's in the bedroom. I'll be right back."

She eyed the tiny tree on his counter. The one she'd given him, using his own argument against him, saying it was hypocritical to be part of a Christmas tree farm and not have a Christmas tree.

"You know—" Hawkins' voice echoed from the other room "—I've been thinking." He appeared, holding a small gift bag. "Well, more like wondering." He stopped in front of her. "If you might be interested in another type of collaboration."

She was curious, to say the least. Their current collaboration had played out so well. "Possibly." She looked up at him. "What did you have in mind?"

"It's something that includes the two of us, of course."

"Of course."

"And Olivia," he added.

Okay, that one had her lifting a brow.

"And maybe," he continued, "another baby or two."

Was he…?

She felt her eyes widen as he dropped to one knee. Her mouth went dry when he reached into the bag and pulled out a small white box. A ring box.

"I would never rush you, Annalise." Staring up at her like she was the most important person in the world, he took hold of her hand. "But I want to make my intentions very clear. I love you with my whole heart, and just the thought of collaborating with you forever and being a father to Olivia makes me the happiest man alive. Will you marry me?"

She couldn't believe it. After all the tears she'd shed in front of him these past few months they'd been together, her eyes were dry as a bone. But oh, there was a certainty in her heart.

"Yes, I will marry you, and I don't care if it's tomorrow or next year. Yes!"

Smiling, he opened the box to reveal the kind of ring she'd always dreamed of. Simple. Elegant. Timeless.

"It's perfect," she said as he slid it on her finger.

Standing, he slipped an arm around her waist and kissed her, sweetly, tenderly.

Suddenly he pulled away. "Wait a minute."

"What is it?"

"You're not crying."

She chuckled. "Like it says in First John, *There is no fear in love.*"

He kissed her once more before saying, "I guess we should get back."

She followed him to the door. "They know, don't they?"

"Of course they do."

Shaking her head, she continued onto the porch.

"By the way," he said as he settled his hand against the small of her back, "I like your options for a wedding. Granted, tomorrow might be a little too soon. However, next year is only a week away."

When they rolled up to Gloriana's a few minutes later, everyone was waiting outside, their expressions no less than expectant.

"I'll come around and let you out," Hawkins said, "and then we'll tell them together."

"Good idea. Leave them wondering a little bit longer."

No one said a word as he made his way around the truck. And when he finally opened her door and helped her out, Annalise held up her left hand.

"I said *yes!*"

Cheers erupted right before they swarmed her and Hawkins.

How blessed she and Olivia would be to be gaining

not only the best husband and father around but also his amazing family.

When someone touched her elbow, Annalise turned to find her mother and father standing behind her. And they were smiling.

"He's a good man," said her father.

"The best."

A tear streaked down her mother's cheek. "And you're an extraordinary woman. I'm so happy for you, Annalise."

Now she was getting weepy. "Thank you, Mom. I had a good teacher." And then right there in front of everyone, her mother hugged her.

Savoring the embrace, Annalise had no idea what had caused her mother to change, only that she was beyond grateful.

"Can we open presents now?"

They all turned to see Kyleigh standing on the porch.

Hawkins moved beside Annalise, slipping an arm around her waist. "I've already received the best gift of all."

While the women chorused *Aww*, Kyleigh said, "Well, that's great for you, Uncle Hawkins, but there are a whole lot of presents under the tree, and I'm gonna lose my mind if we don't open them."

"Well, we can't have that," he responded.

Annalise gathered her daughter as everyone disappeared through the front door. Everyone except Hawkins, who moved beside them.

She looked up at him. "Don't you want to open presents?"

"Why? I've already got the best gifts I could ever

receive." He pressed a kiss to Olivia's head before kissing Annalise.

She'd come to Hope Crossing for a fresh start and to build a legacy for her daughter. Yet what she'd found was so much more. Acceptance. Self-worth. Love. And more happiness than she ever could have imagined.

* * * * *

If you enjoyed this story, be sure to check out the previous book in Mindy Obenhaus's Hope Crossing miniseries:

The Cowgirl's Redemption

Available now from Love Inspired!

Dear Reader,

Thank you for joining me on this second journey to Hope Crossing, Texas. It was fun to revisit some familiar characters and see where life had taken them. Not to mention meet some new faces who just might show up later.

When we first met Hawkins in Gloriana's story, *The Cowgirl's Redemption*, I knew he was a man of honor and could hardly wait to tell his story. But I had to find just the right heroine. And Annalise with her baby girl, Olivia, was the perfect match.

I can relate to Annalise and her feelings of inadequacy. But also like Annalise, I know how the right person can lift you up and give you the courage to do things you never thought possible.

My husband likes to jokingly tell people that he's the inspiration for my stories, but truth be known, he really is. You can imagine his surprise years ago when he found out I was writing a book. Me, the woman who barely read. Yet that didn't stop him from encouraging me every step of the way. Not only does he help me brainstorm my books, he reads every one of them, too.

I hope you have a blessed Christmas season. One filled with the wonder of God's amazing love in the form of a baby born in a manger—Jesus. The greatest gift we could ever receive.

Until we meet again on the pages of my next book, I would love to hear from you. You can contact me via my website, mindyobenhaus.com, or find me on Facebook—just search for *Mindy Obenhaus, author*. And don't forget to sign up for my newsletter so you'll be in the know about book releases and giveaways.

God bless,
Mindy

COMING NEXT MONTH FROM
Love Inspired

HER UNLIKELY AMISH PROTECTOR
by Jocelyn McClay
Amish nanny Miriam Schrock isn't pleased when handsome bad boy
Aaron Raber starts working for the same family as she does. But soon Miriam
sees the good man he's become. When his troubled past threatens them
both, Aaron must step in to protect the only one who truly believes in him...

THE MYSTERIOUS AMISH NANNY
by Patrice Lewis
Lonely Amish widower Adam Chupp needs help raising his young son.
When outsider Ruth Wengerd's car breaks down, she agrees to care for
Lucas until it can be repaired. Ruth fits into Amish life easily but is secretive
about her past. Will Adam learn the truth about her before he loses his heart?

RESTORING THEIR FAMILY
True North Springs • by Allie Pleiter
Widow Kate Hoyle arrives at Camp True North Springs to heal her grieving
family, not the problems of camp chef Seb Costa. But the connection the
bold-hearted chef makes with her son—and with her own heart—creates a
recipe for love and hope neither one of them expects.

THE BABY PROPOSAL
by Gabrielle Meyer
After his brother's death, Drew Keelan finds himself guardian of his infant
nephew. But to keep custody, Drew must get married fast! He proposes a
marriage in name only to the baby's aunt, Whitney Emmerson. But when
things get complicated, will love help keep their marriage going?

RECLAIMING THE RANCHER'S HEART
by Lisa Carter
Rancher Jack Dolan is surprised when his ex-wife, Kate, returns to town and
tells him that they are still married. He suggests that they honor the memory
of their late daughter one last time, then go their separate ways. This could
be the path to healing—and finding their way back to each other...

THE LONER'S SECRET PAST
by Lorraine Beatty
Eager for a fresh start, single mom Sara Holden comes to Mississippi to
help redo her sister's antique shop. And she needs local contractor
Luke McBride's help. But the gruff, unfriendly man wants nothing to do with
Sara. Can she convince him to come out of seclusion and back to life?

**LOOK FOR THESE AND OTHER LOVE INSPIRED BOOKS WHEREVER
BOOKS ARE SOLD, INCLUDING MOST BOOKSTORES, SUPERMARKETS,
DISCOUNT STORES AND DRUGSTORES.**

LICNM1122

Get 4 FREE REWARDS!

We'll send you 2 FREE Books <u>plus</u> 2 FREE Mystery Gifts.

FREE Value Over **$20**

Both the **Love Inspired®** and **Love Inspired® Suspense** series feature compelling novels filled with inspirational romance, faith, forgiveness, and hope.

YES! Please send me 2 FREE novels from the Love Inspired or Love Inspired Suspense series and my 2 FREE gifts (gifts are worth about $10 retail). After receiving them, if I don't wish to receive any more books, I can return the shipping statement marked "cancel." If I don't cancel, I will receive 6 brand-new Love Inspired Larger-Print books or Love Inspired Suspense Larger-Print books every month and be billed just $6.24 each in the U.S. or $6.49 each in Canada. That is a savings of at least 17% off the cover price. It's quite a bargain! Shipping and handling is just 50¢ per book in the U.S. and $1.25 per book in Canada.* I understand that accepting the 2 free books and gifts places me under no obligation to buy anything. I can always return a shipment and cancel at any time by calling the number below. The free books and gifts are mine to keep no matter what I decide.

Choose one: ☐ **Love Inspired**
Larger-Print
(122/322 IDN GRDF)

☐ **Love Inspired Suspense**
Larger-Print
(107/307 IDN GRDF)

Name (please print)

Address   Apt. #

City   State/Province   Zip/Postal Code

Email: Please check this box ☐ if you would like to receive newsletters and promotional emails from Harlequin Enterprises ULC and its affiliates. You can unsubscribe anytime.

> **Mail to the Harlequin Reader Service:**
> **IN U.S.A.:** P.O. Box 1341, Buffalo, NY 14240-8531
> **IN CANADA:** P.O. Box 603, Fort Erie, Ontario L2A 5X3

Want to try 2 free books from another series! Call 1-800-873-8635 or visit www.ReaderService.com.

---

*Terms and prices subject to change without notice. Prices do not include sales taxes, which will be charged (if applicable) based on your state or country of residence. Canadian residents will be charged applicable taxes. Offer not valid in Quebec. This offer is limited to one order per household. Books received may not be as shown. Not valid for current subscribers to the Love Inspired or Love Inspired Suspense series. All orders subject to approval. Credit or debit balances in a customer's account(s) may be offset by any other outstanding balance owed by or to the customer. Please allow 4 to 6 weeks for delivery. Offer available while quantities last.

Your Privacy—Your information is being collected by Harlequin Enterprises ULC, operating as Harlequin Reader Service. For a complete summary of the information we collect, how we use this information and to whom it is disclosed, please visit our privacy notice located at corporate.harlequin.com/privacy-notice. From time to time we may also exchange your personal information with reputable third parties. If you wish to opt out of this sharing of your personal information, please visit readerservice.com/consumerschoice or call 1-800-873-8635. **Notice to California Residents**—Under California law, you have specific rights to control and access your data. For more information on these rights and how to exercise them, visit corporate.harlequin.com/california-privacy.

LIRLIS22R2

HARLEQUIN
PLUS

Announcing a **BRAND-NEW** multimedia subscription service for romance fans like you!

Read, Watch and Play.

Experience the easiest way to get the romance content you crave.

Start your **FREE 7 DAY TRIAL** at
<u>www.harlequinplus.com/freetrial</u>.

HARPLUS0822

Inspired by true events,
The Secret Society of Salzburg
**is a gripping and heart-wrenching story of
two very different women united to bring
light to the darkest days of World War II.**

Don't miss this thrilling and uplifting page-turner
from bestselling author

RENEE RYAN

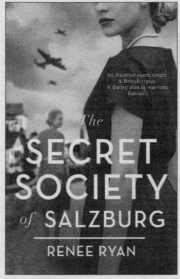

An Austrian opera singer.
A British typist.
A daring plan in war-torn
Europe.

THE
SECRET
SOCIETY
of SALZBURG

RENEE RYAN

"A gripping, emotional story of courage and strength,
filled with extraordinary characters."
—*New York Times* bestselling author **RaeAnne Thayne**

Coming soon from Love Inspired!

LOVE INSPIRED
LoveInspired.com

LI42756BPA